Brawler

I0534195

Low Blow #3

Charity Parkerson

--Warning: This book is intended for readers over the age of 18.

Introduction

It'll take one hell of a brawler to fight through this mess. Luckily, Aden is used to uphill battles.

At one time, Aden was one of the most sought after trainers in the world. Unfortunately, he folded under the pressure. Now he lives the quiet life in Key Largo, running a small but exclusive gym. When he walked away from his old life, he did so with no regrets sans one—Remy Bergeau, the current welterweight champion.

Remy and Aden have history. That's the best way Remy can describe the way Aden destroyed his life, leaving his heart and reputation in tatters. Remy might be bitter, but he's not much on holding a grudge. When his sponsors send him to Key Largo for a photo-op, Remy has no plan beyond getting in and out with his pride intact. Nothing could prepare him for seeing Aden again.

No one has ever made Aden want to set a match to the kindling of his life like Remy. All it takes is five minutes in the man's company for Aden to do just that—revealing his every secret. Now, all Aden can do is hope the truth will set Remy free long enough for Aden to recapture the man's heart.

Chapter 1

Brawler: An aggressive fighter who likes to fight on the inside.

He was wearing eyeliner. Remy Bergeau had always been eccentric. That wasn't why Aden was currently running his tongue over his teeth and fighting back homicidal tendencies. Equally, it had nothing to do with every man in his training center flocking to get Remy's autograph instead of working on the individual assignments Aden had set for them. Well, except for Gunnar. That dude was staring at the opposite wall, carefully avoiding looking at Remy, while taking his pent-up rage out on one of Aden's bags. Like Gunnar, Aden and Remy had history, and it wasn't a good one. Aden watched Remy smile like he was on stage while signing everything shoved under his nose. As welterweight champ, he wasn't a big guy. That didn't matter when a man had been fighting his whole life. Someone as flamboyant as Remy had definitely been holding his own since birth. At one time, Aden had respected the hell out of Remy—skinny jeans, hair gel, and eyeliner aside. Of course, at one time, Aden had also respected himself. Those days were gone for them both.

It wasn't every day that fighters in training got to meet the big names. By now, Gunnar's novelty had worn off with the other men. That was the only reason Aden let this shit go on at all. His men needed to see people who'd made it to the top, so they wouldn't stop pushing and dreaming it could happen to them. It only took five minutes before he couldn't take anymore. Bringing his fingers to his mouth, Aden let out an ear-piercing whistle, calling his men back under control and sending them scrambling. Remy's steel blue eyes slid Aden's way. He didn't smile, but Aden knew in his heart Remy was laughing at him.

"Still a hard ass, I see."

Son of a bitch. He'd forgotten the thick New Orleans accent. It was near to being old world southern—like Remy stepped out of a dream.

"My office. Now."

"Mmm, yes," Remy said, each syllable coming out in a purr as he moved to do as told. "Definitely still a harsh taskmaster. You know how much I like the rough stuff."

Aden ground his back teeth when several curious eyes moved their way. The last thing Aden needed or wanted was any rumors starting up about Remy and him. As of now, Gunnar still spoke to him. Remy moved past Aden, heading inside Aden's office as if he'd been there a hundred times rather than not at all. Aden's gaze automatically dropped to Remy's ass as he passed. He considered ripping his eyes out when he realized what he'd done. Goddamn it. It was still the sexiest ass on the planet.

"Why are you here?" Aden asked the instant the door snapped closed behind them. The barely suppressed growl to his voice was something Remy would have to deal with. It didn't matter his anger wasn't Remy's fault.

Remy ignored him, doing as he pleased, as always. He trailed his fingertips along Aden's desk without glancing Aden's way. "I remember this desk well. It's hard to believe you brought it with you from New Orleans, but I'd recognize it anywhere." Turning, Remy hopped up onto the edge and flashed Aden a cheeky grin. His dimples made an appearance, competing with the mischief in Remy's eyes for top marks in the wicked department. "The first time you fucked me was on this desk. I don't remember it being this hard." He winked. "Of course, I was more concerned with your wood than this piece."

"Why are you here?" Aden repeated. His voice had gone husky, the way it always did when Remy was involved. Unlike Remy, Aden remembered exactly how hard everything had been that night. Hell would freeze and he'd be carrying around the remnants of his desk in a matchbox before he'd consider getting rid of it.

Remy's smiled faded. "I had to see for myself if the rumors were true." Aden didn't take the bait. He didn't want to know. Anything Remy said to him in that hurt tone was a deeper conversation than Aden could handle. Remy didn't need his input to keep going. "After you pulled up stakes and disappeared from New Orleans, I didn't wonder about you at all."

Ouch.

"Anytime anyone spoke your name, I shut them down. I knew, wherever you'd gone, you'd still be training Gunnar." Remy shook his head and a self-deprecating smile shaped his gorgeous lips. "Bitterness has kept me very warm at night. Well, that, and lots of men who—unlike you—have found me to be quite enough to keep them satisfied."

Double ouch.

"But imagine my surprise when I opened *The Daily Sports Review* the other day and learned that Gunnar, Boston, and you were all happily living alongside one another in the same small town." Remy enunciated every word, as if hammering nails in Aden's coffin. Remy slid from the desk, looking unfazed by the knowledge, which did nothing to remedy the rapid beating of Aden's heart. "Since I'm on my way to have dinner at Boston's new restaurant and you're hanging out with Gunnar today, I guess I have my answer." Remy headed for the door.

Without thought, Aden stepped into his path, blocking Remy's exit. His brain screamed for him to let Remy go. His heart demanded Aden do something—anything to convince Remy to stay. "Tell me what I can do."

"Nothing." Remy's answer rang true on every level. The man genuinely wanted nothing at all from Aden. It hurt. "Like I said, I just needed to see it for myself." Remy tried stepping around him. Aden refused to budge.

Without a plan, his arm snaked out, snagging Remy's waist. "Don't leave. Not yet." As much as Aden had thought he'd known how deep his self-hatred went, he realized in that moment that he'd known nothing. Aden had always been more than aware of how much he'd lost, but having Remy right there, he couldn't stand by and watch him go.

Remy's gaze was clear of all love, pain, and regrets. He'd let Aden go. Aden could see it. Still, Aden didn't release him. "Did you ever come clean to Gunnar?"

Aden dropped his arm and stepped aside at Remy's question. "Would it change anything?"

"I guess we'll never know," Remy said, sounding overly bright. Aden wondered if Remy would tweak his nose. That's how goddamn fake he sounded.

Something inside Aden snapped. He wasn't a fucking coward. When he'd gone after Remy the first time, he'd done so with everything he had. Even if Remy hated him or never thought of him at all, Aden would still fall at his feet and torch his life. He threw open the door. His gaze locked on Gunnar.

"I need to see you for a second."

Even though Aden kept his tone civil, Gunnar's eyebrows still rose in challenge. "Um, nope. Fuck a bunch of that bullshit. You can talk to me when he leaves."

A growl escaped Aden. "I'm not feckin' playin', Gunnar. Move your ass."

In a show of defiance, Gunnar's jaw hardened. "I pay you. Not the other way around. You need to remember that shit."

Remy swept past Aden. "Don't bother, darling. Unlike you, I'd never expect anyone to damage their reputation or lose a friend on my behalf." Without another word, Remy headed for the door. He didn't spare a glance for Gunnar. With every step the man took, moving away from Aden, Aden diminished a hair. No one else made Aden feel worse than Remy. He brought the sunlight with him when he walked in a room. The sun hadn't shone in Aden's life since the man had walked out of it.

Before Remy reached the door, he stopped to openly flirt with Mateo, one of Aden's prize students. Aden made a mental note to ruin the man's life. A pen appeared and numbers were exchanged. Aden couldn't watch anymore. He slammed his office door closed and paced the perimeter. The floor disappeared beneath his long stride and Aden lost count of the number of passes he made. With every step, his temper darkened.

An old craving rose in Aden's gut. He deserved to hurt.

Without a thought to the consequences, Aden threw the door open once more. He locked gazes with Gunnar and motioned him inside. This time, Gunnar came without argument. Once Gunnar was seated across from him, Aden almost lost his nerve. He honest-to-God didn't know where to start.

Gunnar didn't seem to have the same problem. "Is this where you confess you were sleeping with Remy before your meltdown?"

Aden snorted. "Meltdown," he repeated, testing the word on his tongue. It seemed as good of a word as any to describe a suicide attempt followed up with three months of inpatient rehab. Aden shook it off since that wasn't why he'd called Gunnar into his office. Still, he couldn't let the other half of Gunnar's statement go. "You knew we were sleeping together?" Since Gunnar and Remy had—at one time—been best friends, it shouldn't have surprised Aden, but he'd honestly believed they'd been each other's biggest secret.

Gunnar's expression didn't hold an ounce of judgment or malice. He nodded. "You didn't do a very good job of hiding it. I never pushed Remy to tell me since I knew it could cost you your job with Cornerman Gym.

But I think it's safe to say everyone knew. The way the two of you looked at each other every time you thought no one was watching." Gunnar let out a low whistle. "It was hot enough to strip the paint from the walls."

Aden fought back a blush. He had to clear his throat before responding. "It was a wee bit more than that. Remy was my heart." Aden nearly choked on the words. It was the first time he'd said them to anyone other than Remy. It was also the first time he'd made the admission since taking a lit match to everything he cared about.

To Aden's surprise, Gunnar smiled. "Why did you let him walk out of here, then?"

Against his will, a smile touched Aden's lips. "I admit I wasn't expecting you to say that."

"We're not friends," Gunnar said, surprising Aden with his forthright statement. "When you came here to train me, you made it clear you didn't want to be friends." A bright smile stretched Gunnar's lips. "You've been an unbending thorn in my side and always riding my ass. With your help, I won the title, and you stood up with me at my wedding. Like I said, you're not my friend. You're more like family, and just like with any other family member, maybe I won't like who

14

you end up with, but I'll accept whatever dumbass decision you make." Aden couldn't breathe and he wanted to tell Gunnar to shut the fuck up, but the man kept talking. "If you want to chase after the rotten bastard who called himself my friend while sleeping with Boston behind my back, that's on you. Just don't chase a cheat and expect to catch a saint."

With every word Gunnar spoke, the faster Aden's heart beat. The words burst from Aden's lips. "Remy wasn't the one sleeping with Boston behind your back. I was."

Gunnar blinked. "I'm sorry. What?"

"Aye," Aden said, because he couldn't repeat the confession.

A derisive-sounding snort escaped Gunnar. "That's... what? You're not the one who I found in my house with Boston, so... what?"

Aden held on to the last threads of his calm, pulling them to his chest and hiding his heart. When he spoke, there wasn't an ounce of emotion marring his words. For the first time, Aden sounded every bit as dead inside as he felt. "I don't know what you walked in on with Remy and Boston. By time, I was already in

ICU, barely clinging to life. Pity death was too big of a pussy to take me. Whatever it was, I can't imagine Remy ever hurting you. It was all me."

For a full minute, Gunnar stared at him as if speech was lost to him. Then his spine seemed to give, and he leaned back in his chair, as if losing the will to move. Aden took advantage of the man's silence. No doubt, Gunnar would never give him another chance to explain.

"I was a feckin' junkie, Gunnar. By the time I had the three of you training under me, I'd already created four world champions," he said, holding up four fingers. "The expectations. The pressure. Goddamn, Gunnar. It was a massive weight. Fame is a strange beast," Aden said, because Gunnar was still letting him keep his teeth, and Aden needed it off his chest. "It's a lot like climbing Mount Everest. If you make it to the top without giving up or dying, you feel like you can't breathe and you're so feckin' tired from the climb, you're not sure if you even care you've made it. There's a lucid part of your brain that recognizes you should be happy, but you don't feel it. Everyone expects, once you've done it, it'll be a snap to do a second go around."

Aden swallowed. The confessions tasted worse

than castor oil going down. "I spent more time high than not. Most of my money went up my nose. That's not an excuse. Boston and Remy both had their title bouts on the same night. Remy was upset with me because Cornerman contracts required I be present at the match that would bring the most attention to the gym. That meant I had to go to Boston's. He didn't make a fuss, really. You know Remy. He can be a bit of a ponce, but he doesn't kick up nettles unnecessarily. It was more that it was his big night and he wanted me there."

Even as the worst night of his life spilled from his lips, Aden smiled at the memory of Remy winning that title. No one deserved it more or had held on to it longer. "As you know, they both won."

Gunnar nodded. "I'd been scheduled to fight in New York the night before. The airport closed when they got hit with record snowfall. Boston didn't fuss at all. He said he understood. I couldn't control nature."

Aden nodded. "Yeah. We had two new titleholders, and the party was massive. By the time it spilled back to your place, I had more drugs pumping through my system than I ever had in my life. How I didn't die, I'll never know. Wish I had," Aden said, more to himself.

"I hit the bathroom and downed some pills. For the longest time, I stared at my reflection. Nothing would come into focus. For a little while, I think I forgot where I was. The only thought I had in my head was Remy's fight had ended but he still hadn't called. Everyone was looking at me all the time and I wanted it to stop. I wanted a normal, regular person life. When I opened the bathroom door, I turned the wrong way, and the rooms kept getting darker instead of brighter. My back hit the hallway wall, and a mouth collided with mine. Remy was there with me, and I was over the moon. We were together, and he was kissing me and he'd won the feckin' title."

Aden stopped, because it was all gone and he couldn't keep going down that path. For a moment, he stared at nothing while remembering everything. Silence filled his office. There was only one way to make it stop. "I woke up in the middle of the night and I looked over, searching for Remy, but it wasn't him." Pain clogged Aden's throat. As long as he lived, Aden knew he would never forget the way he'd felt when he'd looked over and seen Boston sleeping next to him.

"How did Remy find out?"

The sound of Gunnar's voice startled Aden. He'd

gotten so lost in his head, he'd forgotten the man was there. "I told him, and then I hopped a plane to Dublin. Well, you know the rest. Two slit wrists later and some much-needed rehab, here I am. You can punch me now if you'd like."

Gunnar shook his head. It was slow, as if he might still be considering it. "I think I just want to go home to Liam. It seems he's the only person I know who isn't a liar." Gunnar came to his feet. His brown hair still clung to his face from his earlier workout, and his blue eyes held a hint of something dark Aden couldn't name. Aden braced himself for anything. "If I don't come back, feel free to take it personally."

*

It only took fifteen minutes to get to Boston's new restaurant, Slip, from Aden's training center. It wasn't nearly enough time to steady Remy's breathing. He didn't know which had been worse—seeing Gunnar or Aden. A loud snort filled the car, breaking the silence. That was a lie. There wasn't enough mental preparation in the world for seeing Aden again. Remy had always been good at hiding his feelings. He'd never had to use so much acting ability in his life. Aden had wrapped an arm around him. The muscles in Remy's stomach clenched at the memory. The man's masculine scent—like something woodsy—had engulfed Remy. Remy's eyes fell closed. He sucked a deep breath through his nose, trying to calm his rage. Remy was so goddamn furious. The anger was all he had anymore. He wrapped it around himself like a security blanket and opened the car door. This was the last place in the world he wanted to be. He had responsibilities to the blessings he'd been given. This was one. He'd suck it up and go inside this fucking place without burning it to the ground. Fucking contractual bullshit making him do things that killed his soul.

As Remy's feet carried him to the door, an unexpected evil grin pulled at the corners of his mouth. It would be fun, though, seeing Boston's face when he walked through the door. Heads turned his way and cell phone cameras appeared. It was almost like walking the damn red carpet just trying to make his way to the hostess for a table. The young blonde woman's eyes lit when they landed on Remy. It was wasted on him, but he'd never turned down a stroke of his ego.

He winked. "Hey there, gorgeous. How hard will it be for me to get a table?"

She beamed. "I could hip check someone out of a

seat for you, if you'd like."

"I'd say he could wait just like everyone else if he wasn't so damn likely to start dancing in the corner, making a spectacle of himself just to hurry us along."

At Boston's sudden appearance, Remy retreated behind a mask of indifference. "You know me well." He really didn't. "It's good to see you, Boston." It really wasn't.

Boston clapped Remy on the back. "It's great to see you too." *Liar.* "This is a long way to come for something to eat."

"I was told anyone who was anyone would be here this weekend for your grand opening. Since I'm here now, it's official; you'll be a smashing success."

"Since you've always turned everything you touch into gold, I'm inclined to believe you," Aden said at Remy's back, stealing the air from Remy's lungs. He was in hell. This was hell. Fuck it. Even burning alive wouldn't keep Remy from being the reigning diva.

"You should both be billionaires, then," Remy said without missing a beat. He could tell by the way Aden winced his jibe had hit home. Remy mentally sharpened his claws, ready for a battle of wits. Daniel Long

21

with *The Daily Sports Report* saved him from himself.

"Remy Bergeau. I need an autograph."

"Shouldn't you have one by now?"

Daniel flashed him a grin. "How about a photograph, then?"

"Oh, babe. You know I'm always up for some time in the spotlight." Daniel's gaze moved past Remy. Remy swore the man practically levitated.

"Aden Dawley. You're an elusive one. I've tried several times to contact your training center and request an interview."

Against his will, Remy's gaze moved Aden's way. He loved to see Aden squirm. Instead of dodging, Aden's face hardened. "I'm not running a social parlor out here. Men pay me for training time, not to sit around giving interviews."

Daniel didn't let up. He kept up the line of questioning as if determined to get his story one way or the other, and as if they weren't crowding the entry of Boston's restaurant. "You've trained seven world champion boxers in your career. You must be proud to have these two under the same roof with you again."

Aden shifted, looking uncomfortable for the first time. The man had always hated any sort of spotlight. "Aye, I'm proud, but my training had little to do with their success. They're the ones who put in the work. I just barked the orders."

Daniel's smile said he thought Aden was being modest. Remy knew different. Aden honestly didn't think it had been anything other than luck, landing him seven men who'd gone on to win the title.

"Can I get a picture of the three of you together?"

"Of course," Remy said before anyone else had a chance to make excuses. He sounded overly bright, even to his ears, but he knew no one else would notice. No one ever thought him anything but outrageous. In this case, hell would freeze before he let any of these men see him bleed. He eyed the other men expectedly. "Come on, guys. Let's squeeze in tight and let Daniel get his picture before I go." He knew the promise of having him out of their hair would get the pair moving. Boston appeared wary but willing to put on a show. Aden looked... broken. They let Daniel move them into the positions he wanted. He honestly didn't give a fuck where he landed in the picture as long as this trip down memory lane concluded soon. Boston ended up in the middle.

A sardonic-sounding laugh escaped Remy. "This feels familiar—you coming between us."

Boston's muscles tensed beneath the arm Remy had around the man's waist. "I swear to God if you're here to make trouble—"

The flashing of the camera cut off Boston's words and had them pasting on fake smiles for the next round of pictures. The second Daniel was finished, Remy quickly stepped away from Boston, putting the distance between them he needed to save his sanity. He shook Daniel's hand, giving his apologies for heading out early. As soon as he was free from listening ears, Remy focused on Boston. He knew Aden was still standing there, hanging on every word, but Remy was getting tired, and his guard was slipping.

"I'm not here to cause trouble. One of my sponsors asked me to come here and get a photo with all my old pals." Remy heard the sarcasm dripping from that final word, but he couldn't stop. "So here I am. I've done my part in keeping sponsors happy. Now I'm more than ready to let you get on with things."

A deep line appeared between Boston's eyes, as if

he didn't know how to react. "If you don't want to hang around and try out the place, you should stay long enough to meet my husband," Boston said, extending an olive branch.

Something ugly rose from deep inside Remy. It wasn't fair for Boston to have anything good in his life, especially a husband. Of course, Remy had learned long ago life wasn't fair at all when it came to him. He tried shoving it down. "Good luck with your new venture." It was the best Remy could choke out. Without glancing Aden's way or meeting anyone else's eye, Remy headed for the door. He was almost done with this place and these people. No need to ever look back again.

"Remy, hold up."

Remy's steps faltered as he reached his rental car and Aden's voice cut through the air. His eyes fell closed as he tried gathering his strength. He turned, bracing himself against the impact of seeing Aden. It always punched a hole through his chest and squeezed his heart. Even though he'd already seen Aden a few different times tonight, the blow didn't lessen. Aden was almost two of Remy in size. He stood almost a foot taller, making Remy feel tiny. At one time, he'd felt petite and safe, as well as powerful and sexy when Aden was within reach. He'd brought this powerful man to his knees, but then again, hadn't everyone? The reminder had Remy straightening his spine.

"What will people think with both of us running out without eating?"

Aden's brow furrowed in the angry way Remy found so fucking sexy. "Who gives a shit what anyone thinks? I'm not here for Boston. Neither are you, right? Or are you? First, you're here to see for yourself if the rumors are true. Next I hear, you're in town to keep sponsors happy. Which is it?"

"Maybe it's both," Remy said with a wink before adding, "Perhaps it's neither. You should spend some time wondering if anything I say is true. It'll do your soul some good. After all, I've had to spend the last few years weighing every word you ever said to me and wondering if any of it was true."

Aden didn't take the bait. "I know you don't care and it's too late, but I'm sorry for everything—for me."

Remy's rage had him unintentionally showing his heart. "Are you? Because I don't think you realize how your sorry state looks to me."

Aden didn't as much as flinch. "It looks like I kept living my life, as if I didn't destroy yours."

Okay. Maybe Aden did realize how it looked. Remy did what he always did under pressure—hid behind humor. "Bitch, please. You can't destroy me. I'm fucking fabulous."

Aden didn't smile and Remy didn't know why he'd tried to make him. That was a lie. Aden rarely smiled and never laughed. When he did, it was like rainbows and all the happy, shiny shit Remy loved. The world felt right. That didn't happen often for Remy. He was outrageous because life was joke and fit like a bad suit. When Aden had loved him, Remy had belonged somewhere for the first time in his life. It had all been a lie.

"No one could ever dim your light, my heart. You are feckin' fabulous."

All the humor inside Remy died at Aden's endearment and serious tone. "I probably won't ever see you again."

"Aye," Aden said. The word came out in barely a whisper.

Remy fiddled with his keys and cast a desperate look around the parking lot. He didn't owe Aden anything. Perhaps he owed himself some peace of mind by saying something he should have a long time ago.

"I loved you, you know?"

A deep line appeared between Aden's eyes as if he barely stopped himself from flying into a rage. "Aye."

Remy chewed his bottom lip, wondering what he could live with and what he couldn't. "It was never much of a consolation to me, but—like most everyone—Boston didn't know we were together. He didn't know he'd destroyed something..." Remy cleared his throat, incapable of finishing.

"Boston's a chancer."

He was, but it didn't matter. It would never matter how horrible of a person Boston was because at the end of the day—no matter what Boston hadn't known—Aden had known what he was ruining, something beautiful. Without another word, Remy unlocked the car's door and slid behind the wheel. The tiny sports car the rental agency had given him suited him. It was red and flashy. Remy like shiny things, and red things, for that matter. He tried focusing on anything other than leaving Aden—his gorgeous red-haired giant.

Before Remy could close the door, Aden surprised him by going down onto his knees on the pavement inside the open door. With Aden in the way, Remy couldn't close the door to leave.

"I'm genuinely sorry for everything, Remy."

Remy couldn't stop staring at the green eyes he'd fallen in love with.

"Not just Boston," Aden continued, as if Remy wasn't dry drowning. "But every feckin' thing I ever did that made you feel like anything less than the bright twinkling star you are. This isn't me, on my knees, begging for forgiveness. This is me, on my knees, begging you to never stop being the class clown."

Remy's throat swelled. He couldn't respond.

Aden kept talking and saved him from trying. "You are laughter and light in the darkest goddamn world. It's okay if you never forgive me or think of me again. Just don't stop being you." Aden came to his feet and closed Remy's door before walking away. Aden swiped at his eyes, and hot tears threatened to spill over Remy's lashes. There was only one way to shore up the cracks reopening in his heart. Remy needed to buy some red shoes to match his car. Fucking Aden, threatening to ruin his mascara in a town where there wasn't a single goddamn shoe store.

Chapter 2

Early morning as the sun broke the sky was Aden's favorite time of the day. He loved unlocking the doors of his training center and taking in the silence. This morning, his back reminded him of the passage of time. Every muscle pulled tight when he moved. The ring was the perfect place to stretch out and extend each muscle. Aden wasted no time moving toward the center and going down onto his back. As he stared at the ceiling, the steel beams were replaced with the memory of Remy's face before he'd driven away the night before. When the man had waltzed in here, he'd been free of all emotion. It was a mask. Right before Remy had driven away, that façade had fallen away. Aden wished he hadn't seen what lay beneath. There was something ugly living inside Remy now. Aden had tainted something beautiful. He wasn't sure if he could live with that. After Gunnar walked away, Aden hadn't lasted five minutes before he was right behind him. At the time, all he'd wanted was to catch Remy before the man left town, say he was sorry, and move on. Now he knew the truth. He'd never move on.

"You're still an early morning person, I see."

Aden's head jerked up at the sound of Remy's voice. "I thought you were leaving town?"

Remy leaned his arms on the rope surrounding the ring and set his chin on his forearm. "My flight back isn't until tomorrow morning."

He couldn't stop his gaze from eating up every nuance of Remy. The eyeliner was still in place. "When you said you were sent for a photo op, I thought that's why you were finally wearing eyeliner in public, but it's back today. Is this your new style?"

A wicked smile touched Remy's lips, and he winked. "Just embracing my many quirks. Do you not like it?"

There was nothing about Remy Aden didn't like. "You should already know how I feel about you getting dolled up. It suits you." Even Aden heard the longing in his voice. Clearing his throat, Aden rolled onto his knees and took in Remy's attire. He wore workout pants and a V-neck tight-fit T-shirt. "Are you here to work out? You know this place is members only and I charge a massive fee."

Remy rolled his eyes before taking a step back and spreading his arms wide. "Name's Chad. Chad does Crossfit. Crossfit Chad doesn't need your high-priced help staying ripped." The man did such a damn good impression of a conceited gym rat that a burst of laughter escaped Aden. Remy's infectious smile grew wider, reminding Aden of an important fact about the man. Remy was a showboat who fed on laughter. Tucking his arms, Remy pulled off a flawless hands-free cartwheel before stamping his foot like a sumo wrestler. "Crossfit Chad is also a vegan. You can't teach this level of awesome."

The laughter reverberating off the walls of the otherwise empty gym sounded out of place. Aden couldn't stop. Even as he shook with humor, a pain sliced through his chest, reminding Aden of all he'd lost. "Let's tape up those fists and see a demonstration of this awesomeness you speak of."

Remy didn't dim. "You're on."

After rolling from the ring, Aden grabbed the tape and moved to help Remy get ready to box. He was halfway through wrapping Remy's second hand before his motions slowed. Doing this for his men was such a habit, it had become second nature. Now the impact of touching Remy again set in. Aden didn't want to stop. He smoothed out the final piece across Remy's knuckles. His pulse beat in his ears. Aden kept his gaze locked on his task. When he couldn't find a reason to drag the moment out any longer, Aden reluctantly dropped Remy's hand and took a step back.

"Let's find you some gloves." As he said the words, Aden finally met Remy's stare. The man's eyes were so goddamn beautiful. Aden had to look away again. He rushed through helping Remy into a pair of gloves before grabbing his punch mitts. Aden knocked the pieces of leather-covered foam together, signaling Remy should start.

Remy's expression transformed from playful to hardened in an instant. Like that, Aden stared at the titleholder. While switching between bouncing on his toes and planting his feet, Remy landed solid blows almost too quick to follow. Pride swelled in Aden's chest. Remy wasn't a case of luck and timing. He was talented and hard working. Every accomplishment Remy had made he deserved. Lost in thought and regret, Aden didn't see the hit coming. Remy bypassed the mitts, dipping low and hitting Aden in the stomach. It didn't hurt, which was the first clue it hadn't been an accident. Remy had pulled his punch. The man's smile was Aden's second clue.

"You're a slick little bastard."

Remy pulled off another flawless flip before coming

at Aden swinging. He purposely missed the mitts several times, landing playful hits to Aden's arms and sides. "Crossfit Chad can kick an old man's ass."

The overwhelming happiness choked Aden. He couldn't stop smiling or hurting. Once upon a time, every day had been like this. Tomorrow, it would be gone again. He didn't think he was a glass-half-empty kind of guy, but this reminder of all he was missing was crippling.

"Settle down there, spider monkey."

Kung Fu noises filled the air as Remy did the opposite of Aden's suggestion. Aden's stomach shook with laughter and the weight of the mitts seemed more like iron and became too much until he dropped his arms, giving in.

Remy bounced away, smiling like the idiot he was. "Do you admit defeat?" His mouth didn't move in time with his words like a bad Kung Fu movie.

Aden shook his head because Remy was ridiculous. A snort escaped him. "Absolutely. You're too much for me."

Remy's smile fell. A flash of something dark crossed over the man's features. "I'm too much for everyone."

Fire lashed through Aden's throat. He wanted to say something—anything to bring the smiles back. As always, he was useless.

"Damn. Look what we have here. This is something I haven't seen in an age. Two of my favorite workout buddies together again."

Aden's gaze shot Gunnar's way at the man's appearance. Remy didn't turn. His stare bored into Aden, demanding Aden's focus.

The moment Remy had Aden's attention, he dipped his chin. "It was nice seeing you, darling. Crossfit Chad's got places to be." Without a backward glance or as much as turning his head in Gunnar's direction, Remy pulled off his gloves and tossed them aside before heading for the door. All Aden could do was watch him go in helpless silence. Aden's gaze slid Gunnar's way. He couldn't play witness to Remy walking away from him again. His heart would know when it was over without his eyes seeing it happen. Gunnar stared at him in a way that hurt almost as much—like he could read Aden's thoughts. Aden cleared his throat. "You showed up."

Gunnar didn't accept the topic change. "Go after him. If not, you'll regret it."

"I can't fix it."

"You can't break it either," Gunnar said, pointing out the obvious.

"He's leaving in the morning."

Gunnar shrugged. "It's not like he lives on another planet." Gunnar snorted before adding, "Even though he acts like he's from the planet of dumbassary. Still, there's nothing stopping you from chasing him as far as he runs."

Aden glanced around at the new life he'd built for himself. "You're on the feckin' clock, Gunnar. Why are you standing around nattering on like an old marm? Let's get you taped up."

Gunnar shook his head. "You're an idiot."

"That's always been true," Aden agreed as he found the tape he'd used earlier for Remy. "I'm not likely to change anytime soon."

"You're not even going to ask why I chose to come back, are you?"

Aden kept his gaze locked on wrapping Gunnar's hands. "You've always been too nice for your own good."

"Liam made me come back."

A snort escaped Aden. "You also married someone too nice for his own good."

"He is nice," Gunnar agreed. "But he's also smart. He reminded me of a few important details. Boston is...

37

Boston. If he hadn't been a miserable, cheating bastard, I wouldn't have come back here to this town where I grew up and reconnected with the love of my life."

Against his will, Aden couldn't stop staring at Gunnar's smile. He looked so certain of every word he spoke.

"Sometimes, Aden, you have to make horrible mistakes before you can fully appreciate someone amazing. I can't spend any more of my life worrying about the past. Before yesterday, I didn't know about you and Boston, and it didn't hurt me when you told me. It seems a bit stupid to get pissed off about it now. I think we were all different people back then." Gunnar's face screwed up in thought as Aden slipped gloves over his taped knuckles. "Except maybe not Remy," Gunnar added. "From what I witnessed when I walked in, he seems to be the same ridiculous guy he's always been."

Without thought, Aden's mouth lifted in one corner. Goddamn. His chest hurt. He missed Remy. "Let's get started."

Gunnar didn't budge. "You won't give an inch, will you?"

Aden snagged his punch mitts from where he dropped them earlier. "What would you have me say, Gunnar? You should hate me. So too should Remy. If I could wave a magic wand and take back that night, I would in a heartbeat. If you're needing my blood here, then fine. Remy was the one for me. I don't know if people get more than one, but I won't be searching for another."

"Go after him. I'll take over training for you until you get back."

Gunnar's offer meant more than Aden could express for more reasons than the man would ever know, but it was too late. "Thank you for the offer."

"But no thanks. Is that what you're saying?" Without waiting for an answer, Gunnar jumped in Aden's ass with both feet. "You know what your problem is? You don't care to find out if it's too late," Gunnar answered, once again not giving Aden time to speak. "This isn't about Remy, or me, or Boston—for that matter— any longer. It's you, punishing yourself. Let me tell you something. You can be as hard as you want for the rest of your life, but it won't make up for the times when you were weak."

Aden wanted to deny Gunnar's words. He couldn't,

but it was also his choice. "Remy deserves someone better than me."

Gunnar snorted before flipping his eyes to the ceiling and releasing a loud sigh. "I don't fucking know why I'm arguing for either of you. Do what you want. If you decide you want to run after him, then my offer still stands. If not, what the fuck ever. I'm fine to never talk about this again."

Awesome. Aden could go back to being dead inside. Just as he deserved.

*

Remy's heart raced. It also screamed for him to turn around, go back inside Aden's training center, and steal a few more minutes with Aden. His feet kept moving. He hadn't felt so alive in years. Now Gunnar was here, and the moment was gone. Remy stood with his hand on the door handle of his car for way longer than he intended as the memory of Aden's laughter rang through his head. He'd forgotten how it had felt to make Aden happy. The man barked and growled at everyone; everyone except Remy. The more obnoxious Remy behaved, the angrier Aden should get. Instead, Remy's ridiculousness fed something inside Aden no one else saw. The moment Gunnar had shown up,

Remy had known their moment was over. Aden would retreat and so would Remy. They were only real when they were alone together.

Time slipped away as Remy slid behind the wheel of his rental. For as long as Remy lived, he would never forget the first time he'd seen Aden unguarded.

The training center had been empty of all other patrons for close to an hour. Remy liked staying late. When everyone left, and he had the place to himself, he felt like an overachiever. For him, that was a good thing and a matter of pride. If he never won a title, it wouldn't be because he didn't put the work in.

Aden had been cleaning for over half an hour. No doubt, the giant Irishman couldn't wait for Remy to leave so he could go home. Honestly, Remy didn't know why he continued lingering. He'd finished his session twenty minutes ago.

"Would you like some help?" It wasn't as if Remy had anywhere else to be.

Aden glanced up, surprise etching his features. "Brown-nosing doesn't earn points with me."

A smirk pulled at Remy's lips at Aden's choice of words. "How do you know? You've never had my nose

41

in your ass."

A low chuckle rumbled from Aden, shocking Remy speechless. He'd never seen Aden smile, much less laugh. Damn. It was kind of hot.

"You've been screwing around for the past half hour. Your offer is a wee late. I'm almost done."

Remy didn't want to leave now. He'd heard Aden's laughter, but maybe it had been a fluke. "Oh, I didn't intend to help you clean. My offer was for entertainment purposes. You clean. I entertain." Remy burst into song. "Nobody polishes the way you do." Remy added a Pip slide to his song. "You're the king of wiping down steel." There was no beat or rhyme to Remy's song. His dance moves also didn't match anything, but Aden's smile was firmly in place. The man had a dimple in the apple of his cheek right below his eye. Jesus. It was ridiculously adorable for such a hard man.

"You should stick to boxing."

"You think?" Remy asked, moonwalking.

"Do you have an off switch?"

Remy cupped his hand behind his ear. "What's

that? It's hard to hear over the sound of my awesome-
ness. Did you ask if I like to switch? Not especially. I'm
more of a bottom."

Aden scrubbed his hand over his face as if trying to
wipe away his smile.

Remy pointed at Aden as he moonwalked toward
the door. "You should lock up and get a drink with me."

"You're not supposed to be drinking. You have a
match this weekend."

"Of milk. A drink of milk. Damn. You never let me
finish."

"Are you finished?" Aden asked, sounding serious.

Was he? Remy thought it over. The butterflies danc-
ing in his stomach warned he should walk away now.
The heat in Aden's gaze had Remy's feet glued to the
floor. When Remy didn't move or respond, Aden tossed
his rag aside.

"I have a ton of protein samples in my office. They're
probably not great, but they're free."

"Sounds interesting. Life on the wild side suits you."

"You have low fun standards if you expect protein
gets my blood pumping."

Remy turned the lock on the gym door, officially clos-ing them off from the world. "I meant me. This wild ride will definitely get your blood pumping."

*

Somehow, Aden managed to make it through the day. He only worked three hours on Sunday mornings, and only then for his most prominent clients. Today, he'd barely made it through those one hundred and eighty minutes, except for the ones he'd spent with Remy. His steps slowed as he reached his car. There was a note on his windshield.

"Crossfit Chad has new digits."

Aden bit back a chuckle as he stared at the phone number. It wasn't a New Orleans area code. After sav-ing Remy's info to his phone, Aden opened his search engine and looked up the area code. Nevada. Why did Remy have a Nevada number? Aden stared into space, debating. He couldn't let Remy go. In truth, Aden never really had. Everything Gunnar had said earlier was the truth. Aden deserved years of misery for every ounce of hurt he'd caused, but he couldn't walk away from Remy forever without knowing there was zero chance for them. Digging through his wallet, Aden went in search of the card Daniel Long handed him before he'd run after Remy the night before. When he found it, Aden didn't hesitate to dial the number.

Daniel answered on the third ring. "Hello?"

"It's Aden."

"Did you change your mind about that interview?"

Aden didn't stop to consider if this was a mistake. There was no limit to how far he'd go for Remy. "I'll answer your questions in exchange for some info."

"All right." Daniel didn't hesitate in his agreement. "What sort of information are you looking for?"

"Everything about Remy Bergeau. Where's he living now? Where does he train? Everything."

"Deal."

Satisfaction roared through Aden. It was a small step, but it was in Remy's direction—where Aden belonged.

Chapter 3

There was nothing except a plain and locked steel door with a keypad at the address Daniel had given him. Aden had known No Rival fight club was an exclusive training facility, but he'd been expecting something different. There didn't seem to be a way inside. At a loss, Aden cast a glance around the quiet parking garage, trying to decide what to do. Daniel hadn't had a home address on Remy. All the man had known was Remy now lived somewhere just outside Vegas and was a member of No Rival. He'd only known that much because it had—apparently—been a huge deal. No Rival only trained MMA fighters, but they'd taken on Remy. It was unheard of.

A bald man who matched Aden in size caught Aden's eye as he moved in Aden's direction. He had a gym bag in one hand and a blond toddler balanced on his hip. The man smiled when he caught sight of Aden standing there, no doubt looking lost. He looked nice and somewhat familiar. It wasn't until the man reached Aden's side that recognition hit.

"Drew Alexander," Aden said as a way of greeting. Drew was the world MMA heavyweight champion and owned No Rival. It had been several years since they'd seen each other. Drew hadn't changed much.

Drew's gray eyes flashed with good humor. "Aden Dawley. It's been a long time."

Aden nodded. "It has."

"If you're headed inside, do you mind giving me a hand? Punch 8539 into that keypad, please?"

Aden did as asked, disengaging the lock on the door before holding it open for Drew. "Who's this fella?" Aden asked, nodding toward the toddler as Drew passed.

"This is my youngest, Ethan." At the mention of his name, the little boy held up a toy car for Aden to see.

"That's awesome, wee one."

Drew motioned Aden toward an empty office. "Come on in." He set Ethan on his feet before closing a baby gate across the office door and tossing the gym bag on the floor. Ethan immediately began tearing open the bag, pulling toys, diapers, and clothes out into the floor. "What brings you by?" Drew asked as he settled in behind his desk and waved for Aden to take the seat on the opposite side. "I thought you were off living the beach life somewhere down south."

"And I thought you were only training MMA fighters," Aden shot back. "When did you decide to dip your toe into the boxing scene?"

"Ah, Remy," Drew said, as if all his questions had been answered. "You know I've always been a collector of champions. I met Remy at a charity event a couple of years ago. Remy is an impressive and memorable guy," Drew said with laughter lacing his words. "He was in the market for a new trainer and I was willing to give it a try if he was. We've done well together."

Ethan pulled on Aden's pants leg. Aden automatically lifted the boy into his lap while keeping up his end of the conversation. "I'm glad he's found a good home here."

Drew leaned back in his chair and linked his fingers behind his head while eyeing Aden with open curiosity. "Is this a welfare check of sorts?"

Aden switched his focus to the little boy currently playing with his fingers. Drew's expression was too searching. Aden wasn't ready to give up any answers. "I guess you could call it that."

"Ethan doesn't usually let anyone hold him. He's

too busy tearing the place down."

"Kids have always liked me," Aden said, sounding absent even to his ears. "Back home in Dublin, I have a score of nieces and nephews." Not that any of his three sisters would let him anywhere near their kids anymore. Being a junkie did that to a person's life. It didn't matter he'd been clean for three years. They hadn't forgotten, and he wasn't forgiven.

"Come on, then," Drew said, coming to his feet. "Remy should be around here somewhere and I need to do my rounds, check in on my boys."

Aden came to his feet as well with Ethan still held in his arms. He glanced around, unsure of what to do with him. Even though part of the room had been converted into a playroom, surely Drew didn't intend to leave Ethan alone in the office. Neither did Aden think the child should be toddling around with a bunch of rough fighters. Since Drew wasn't reaching for Ethan, and the boy seemed content enough, Aden held on to him.

He followed on Drew's heels, stepping over the baby gate and heading into the heart of the building. Aden took in every detail of the club. It was clean, but it wasn't high tech. There was a ring, an octagon, and a

49

practice mat for sparring. Different styles of punching bags hung from the ceiling and treadmills lined the walls. It couldn't have been more apparent that Drew stuck to the basics of teaching. Aden's respect for the man grew. He hated all the new age bullshit people used for training. Men faced each other in the ring with nothing but their fists and their pride. No one needed a ten-thousand-dollar machine to teach them how to do that. Aden could also tell the level of professionalism inside the building was off the charts. It was obvious the men recognized how lucky they were to train with the best.

When Remy came into view, Aden's heart sped, but his steps slowed. Focused on his task, Remy didn't turn at their approach. If Drew said a word to Aden, Aden didn't hear him. The pounding of his pulse drowned out everything. He'd never seen Remy look so serious. It was unnerving—like it wasn't him. The club disappeared around Aden as he watched Remy. His punches hit their mark every time. Remy's sleek muscles moved in time with his every punch, reminding Aden of the nights they'd spent together. Remy's muscles had been covered in sweat then too. Aden's gaze swept down Remy's body, measuring and calculating.

"Your footwork is getting lazy."

Remy froze. His arms dropped to his sides. He turned his head, meeting Aden's gaze. If he was surprised to see Aden, he didn't show it. "Is that so?"

Without realizing what he was doing, Aden sucked a deep breath through his nose as Remy's sexy accent rolled over him. He held Remy's stare and nodded. "Do you mind?" he asked Drew while barely sparing a glance for the man standing next to him.

"Go for it," Drew said, reclaiming his son and freeing Aden to climb into the ring.

Aden tried not to think about the body he touched as he repositioned Remy's hips. Dropping to his knees, he readjusted Remy's footing. "Love the shoes," Aden said without thought.

"You know red is my favorite color," Remy shot back. Laughter sounded heavily in his voice as he added, "Especially when I'm staring down at it."

Aden glanced up, meeting Remy's gorgeous stare. His mouth quirked. "I'm sure." After coming to his feet, Aden stood hip to hip with Remy, mimicking his pose. This lesson wasn't only a reminder to Remy but a demonstration for the other men watching as well. After all, Aden was a trainer at heart. He made a quick show of the exact steps he expected Remy to make. "You can't let yourself get lazy in your footwork," he said, rocking forward and throwing a fake punch before bouncing back on his heels. "Throwing a punch isn't everything. You also must be able to withstand getting hit. If you're unbalanced, you'll get knocked on your arse." He demonstrated the move once more before dipping out of the ring and getting out of the way. "Don't get knocked on your arse, Remy." This time, as Remy swiped at the punch mitts, his footwork was perfect. "There you go," Aden said, cheering him on.

Ethan tugged on Aden's sleeve and he let the boy change hands once more while keeping his gaze locked on Remy. As always, he was so damn proud. Everything Remy did impressed him. After a minute, Remy backed away and headed for the ropes. His wicked expression had Aden's feet frozen to the floor. Remy dipped his head through the ropes and blew a raspberry on Ethan's chubby cheek, making the boy giggle. Aden's breath caught in his throat with Remy right there, inches away. His eyeliner was missing today. Aden didn't realize he'd said the words aloud until Remy focused on him. "The people here don't accept me the way you do." Before Aden saw the move coming, Remy swept past Ethan and pressed a quick kiss to Aden's lips before moving away just as fast.

He pointed both arms Aden's way as he walked backward and raised his voice to be heard above the noise inside the club. "Tell the class why you got kissed."

Aden shook his head. "I have no idea."

Remy's luminous smile fell. "That's why it'll never happen again."

Aden scrambled to fix it and bring Remy's smile back. "You kissed me, because all your kisses belong to me, my heart." The bright smile snapped back into place before Remy turned around and returned to his training session. For a moment, the world had fallen away. With Remy's back to him, Aden came back to reality, and he realized how big of an audience they had. He turned his head and found Drew leaned against the ring's corner with his arms crossed over his chest, staring at Aden.

"Things just got real interesting around here." Aden forced down a blush. Drew straightened and reclaimed Ethan. "Stay as long as you'd like. You're obviously a good influence on Remy. I need to get some work done."

Aden nodded, more grateful than he could express. "Thank you."

Drew winked. "Don't thank me yet. I'm a plotter and you've given me ideas."

Even though Aden had no idea what Drew meant, he had a bad feeling he'd eventually find out.

*

Aden was there. Remy was ready to call it a day and find out what the fuck was going on, but he knew Aden wouldn't let him fuck up his routine, even for his benefit. He'd kissed Aden. Jesus. Even Remy didn't know what had come over him. Life and the past had looked a little different—a bit clearer—since he'd left Key Largo. He'd spent so long unwilling to give Aden a chance to really apologize or given himself permission to think about those days. For the past few days, he had allowed himself to have those thoughts—remember every detail. When he looked back, things didn't hurt as much as they had, but the love he'd felt for Aden—that shit hadn't faded at all. Was it total bullshit to love someone who'd cheated on him? Fuck yeah, it was. The thing was—Aden was the one.

Chances were better than not they'd never be to-gether again. Remy had a new life in Vegas. Aden had built a real life in Key Largo. They were worlds apart from each other in every way now. That didn't mean Remy had to hold on to his anger or they couldn't try to be friends again. Remy really wanted to be friends again. Life here in Vegas; it was lonely.

Not only was Aden there, but he stayed all day. He corrected Remy on the little things he'd forgotten since switching trainers. Aden also helped a few of the MMA fighters. It was obvious he couldn't stop himself from doing so. By the time Remy had done as much as he could do, he was ready to crawl out of his skin and was dancing in place.

Carter, Remy's usual training partner, obviously hit his limit. "What's up with you today? You're always a nut, but you're bouncing off the walls."

"Sorry," Remy said, trying to dial it down.

Carter laughed. "I swear, you're like a kid someone gave too much sugar. Have you ever been tested for ADHD?"

Remy bit the inside of cheek. He knew he shouldn't take it personally, but damn. "Sorry," Remy said again.

Aden appeared from nowhere. "Why are you apologizing?"

Remy tried for a fake smile and failed. "No reason."

A deep line formed between Aden's eyes. For some reason, the man's irritation brought a real smile to Remy's face. Aden's gaze moved between Remy and Carter before landing on Remy once more. "Better feckin' be for no reason."

Remy's smile grew until his cheeks ached. He didn't spare another glance for Carter. "Are you ready to get out of here?"

"Aye. Just let me pop by Drew's office and thank him for letting me hang out today."

Remy shook his head. "He's probably already gone. Drew only comes by for a couple of hours a day now. His wife, Aubree, is pregnant with their third kid, and he's all daddy all the time nowadays. I think he's preparing all of us for his eventual backing away from training altogether."

"That's fine. I'll catch him tomorrow."

Even as Remy headed for the door, he kept his gaze locked on Aden. "You're coming again tomorrow?"

"Aye."

Remy had told himself he didn't care why Aden had shown up, but it wasn't true. "Why?"

"You're amazing and everything you touch is gold, my heart, but you're weakening on some things you ought not be weakening on," Aden said, being painfully honest as always. "You've got a match around the corner, and while I think you'll win, I also think it's only a matter of time till you lose if you keep heading down this path."

"So you came twenty-six hundred miles to keep me from losing a match?"

Aden smirked as they stepped outside. Remy's face went numb. Longing hit like an evil, sneaky bitch, sucker punching Remy in the gut. "No. I'm coming back tomorrow to keep you from losing a match. The twenty-six hundred miles was to tell you I miss that squawking you call singing."

Remy drew back in mock offense. "Are you fucking kidding me? I know you don't mean me. Animals flock to me like a fucking fairytale princess when I burst into song."

"What kind of animals? My guess is wolves and vultures. They think you're dying."

An outraged-sounding gasp left Remy. He didn't mean it, but Aden still took advantage. His mouth covered Remy's before Remy had time to recover. Lust and pain overwhelmed Remy as Aden's tongue filled Remy's mouth. Remy's fingers slipped through Aden's locks before tightening on them and holding the man in place. He'd intentionally forgotten this. The Irish brogue that tinged Aden's words, Remy had always sworn he could feel that same vibration in the man's kiss. He sucked dick the same, and Remy's cock knew it. His erection was trying to climb out of his workout shorts and there was no stopping it. Dark thoughts crept in, threatening to cripple him. Had Aden kissed Boston like this? Had Boston felt that small vibration and been brought to his knees? Flattening his palms against Aden's hard chest, Remy pushed. His sanity couldn't withstand this.

Aden didn't look angry or disappointed. His expression was so much worse than that. His eyes screamed his love. Remy couldn't speak from the pain strangling him. "Tell the class why you got kissed," Aden said, mimicking Remy's earlier words.

Remy shook his head, incapable of sharing his thoughts.

"That's why it'll keep happening."

To keep from crying, Remy cleared his throat. "Where are you staying while you're in town?" Yep. That was his voice that sounded husky, giving away how turned on he was. There was nothing for it. Aden had always been his biggest weakness.

Aden shrugged. "My bags are still in my rental car. I figured I'd find the club first and then search for the closest hotel. Any suggestions?"

My place. Remy swallowed back the words. "Um," he said, trying to buy time for his clouded thoughts. "The Rainforest Palace is close by and nice. It's kind of pricey, though."

"I'm not worried about the money. How close is it to you?"

"The hotel is about two miles from here," Remy said, dodging.

"It's okay," Aden said, sounding sad. "You don't have to avoid my question. If you don't want to tell me where you live, you don't have to." Aden took a step back. "I'll see you tomorrow." Aden took another step back. It felt like a mile.

Remy moved forward, filling the gap between them. "Meet me later." He didn't know where the offer came from. All Remy knew was he couldn't let Aden get away.

"Anything you want."

Remy's growing panic soothed at Aden's immediate agreement. "How about you text me when you find out your room number? I'll come fetch you."

"Do I get to know where we're going?"

"I thought you said anything I want."

"Aye. I did. Just wondering what I should wear," Aden said with humor lacing his words.

A burst of laughter rose in Remy. Aden never dressed up for anything other than weddings and funerals. Even then, it was iffy. "Did you bring anything other than jeans, T-shirts, and something to work out in?"

"Nope."

"That's what I thought." Talking about clothes reminded Remy of an important detail. "Fuck. We were so busy talking, I forgot to stop by my locker and grab my bag. Head over and get checked in. I'll grab my bag and catch up with you when know which room you're in."

"I can head back inside with you," Aden said, obviously as unwilling to let Remy out of his sight as Remy was to let go of Aden.

"It's fine. Go. I'll be along soon. Promise," he added when Aden didn't budge.

"All right." Even though Aden sounded reluctant, he did back away. "I'll see you later tonight."

Remy nodded before jogging back inside. He ignored the sensation of Aden's gaze following his every move until he disappeared into the building. With his brain locked firmly on making the perfect plans for the evening, he almost crashed headlong into Carter. He pulled to a quick stop.

Carter didn't smile or tell him to slow the fuck up. "I thought you left," he said, sounding bland.

Remy held up his backpack. "Forgot my bag."

"Are you coming in at your usual time tomorrow?"

Remy dipped his chin by way of answering. He didn't know what was going on with Carter, but the man wasn't overwhelming Remy with the desire to chat. He also wasn't sure where this was headed since he came in at the same time every day. Carter was his usual training partner, but the man wasn't by any means the only person Remy worked with.

"I wasn't sure since you have company in town."

"He's coming with me," Remy said, still trying to decide if this conversation had a purpose and why Carter had such a dick tone happening.

"Great. I guess that means I'll be subjected to another day of you fucking around all day."

Since Remy had gotten every bit as much done today as he did every day, Carter's anger didn't make sense. There was no denying the fury flashing from his blue eyes. "I'm confused."

"I'm not a bit surprised. It's probably because you never focus."

Remy hated arguing, especially when people caught him unawares. The combo left him speechless in the face of Carter's displeasure. He matched Remy in height and build, so Remy wasn't the least bit intimidated. Remy just hated drama.

Carter took a breath as if attempting to call his temper under control. "Take a look around, Remy. Do you see anyone else horsing around? No," Carter answered without waiting for Remy to catch up. "Everyone else here recognizes how goddamn lucky they are to be here. Their work ethic matches that knowledge. They're making sacrifices to be here. But, I guess, since you bought your way in, you're free to focus on your red-haired fuck buddy. I mean, this guy—"

"This guy, what?" Aden asked, sounding deadly as his voice cut through the air. As one, Remy and Carter turned in his direction. Aden and Drew stood in the locker room doorway, wearing matching deadly expressions. "Go on," Aden urged. "I dare you."

Drew took a step forward before Carter had time to lose his teeth. He handed a sleeping Ethan off to Remy. "Hang out for a second, okay?" Drew said as if it was a question when they both knew it was an order. The bald-headed giant focused on Carter. "You. In my office. Now."

Carter held his silence as he did as told.

Remy tried looking anywhere other than at Aden.

"What was that about? Don't lie this time."

Remy nuzzled Ethan's cheek, trying to cling to the child's innocence. Life was so ugly. Ethan smelled like a sweet baby—untainted by it all. "I'm the only boxer here," Remy said. He knew it didn't explain anything to the extent Aden expected, but that was what it all boiled down to. Remy spoke softly, trying not to wake Ethan. "Most of these guys are second or even third generation fighters. They earned their way in by blood, paying with money they can't spare, and hoping for success." Remy shrugged. "A recipe for bitterness." Remy's gaze kept skirting away. He wanted to look at Aden, but he also didn't. "Carter wasn't wrong, though. If I want to be here, I need to match their dedication."

"What the feck? You're the most dedicated person I know."

"I play around too much and lose focus," Remy argued, because it was true.

"That's who you are," Aden said, moving close and leaving Remy no other choice but to hold his stare. "Enjoying what you do doesn't mean you're not working or dedicated. You're a naturally happy person. Don't let anyone steal who you are because they can't achieve what you have."

Remy shook his head, not ready to let it go so easily. "Seriously, he's right. I should focus."

Aden's face screwed up, showing his confusion. "Why do you keep saying that?"

"Because I don't focus," Remy said, sounding desperate even to his ears. "A blind man could see that. If I'd paid more attention to my career than I did you, I could've won the title much earlier." Aden blinked, as if Remy had slapped him, proving the man wasn't hearing him. Remy chose to argue from the other side. "Just like, if I'd focused all my attention on us instead of my career, you wouldn't have needed Boston to fill that gap. It's obvious to everyone I'm failing. I just need to try harder." By the time Remy finished, he rocked from foot to foot. He told himself the motion was for Ethan. In truth, it was to comfort himself. Aden kept staring at Remy as if looking at a stranger, and it was all too much. A panic attack loomed on the horizon.

"All right. This has to stop," Aden said, gently plucking Ethan from Remy's arms. Without another word, knock, or a single excuse me, Aden strolled inside Drew's office and handed him Ethan. "It's time for Remy to go. We'll chat tomorrow."

Remy watched from the doorway, too shocked to

react. Carter kept his face turned carefully away and Drew never looked away from Aden, making Remy wonder if Aden looked every bit as angry as he sounded. Judging by Drew's expression, he didn't know what to say—not that Aden gave him time. Drew tended to give everyone everything they wanted. In exchange, everyone did the same for him. It was apparent Aden was the first person he'd encountered in a long time who didn't give a fuck who Drew was. It was equally obvious that they were leaving. In the wake of baring his soul, all Remy could do was follow along.

"Where's your car?" Aden asked the moment they cleared the door.

"I run here," Remy answered, sounding absent. "As part of my routine," he added. "Two miles here. Two miles home."

Aden maneuvered him toward a gray SUV. It looked the same as every SUV rental ever. "Well, not today. Get in."

Since there was something wrong with Remy's breathing, he let Aden shove him inside the vehicle. Air became harder to come by with every passing moment. The instant Remy's ass hit the seat, Aden reached beneath it and shoved the seat back as far as it would go before pushing Remy's head down between his knees.

"Take a breath, my heart. You're turning colors."

Remy sucked air, trying to slow his heart. "Sorry," Remy said between breaths. He felt like all he did was apologize anymore. "Don't know what happened."

"Too many people staring at you, that's what," Aden said, sounding sure and going a long way toward soothing Remy's panic. Aden closed the door and circled the car before sliding behind the wheel. He didn't immediately turn the ignition. His hand slid down Remy's spine. Remy took another deep breath at the contact. "Where do you live?"

Remy turned his head, meeting Aden's gaze. The man's expression was soft and filled with concern. Remy felt the weight of his loss heavier in that moment than he had in a long time. "Turn left from the parking garage. The Rainforest Palace is in two miles on the right."

Aden's expression transformed into barely suppressed anger. "Are you feckin' kidding me, Remy? I'm trying to take care of you, and still you won't budge a goddamn inch."

In spite of Aden's irritation, a low chuckle slipped

from Remy, surprising even him. He sat up. "I live in one of the upper floor penthouses at The Rainforest Palace."

The immediate blush tinting Aden's cheeks went far at easing the tightness in Remy's chest. "All right. Put your seat belt on."

Remy did as instructed, but his gaze remained locked on Aden. "My penthouse has three bedrooms."

"Where do you sleep? Surely it takes that many rooms just for your shoe collection."

Since Aden was smiling and Remy loved that shit, he let it slide. "I've gotten better at organizing, but that wasn't my point. You should stay with me."

"If that's what you want."

Aden's quick agreement had Remy chewing his bottom lip, trying to hold back the question. He lost the battle. "Why did you come here?"

"Because you're here," Aden answered without hesitation. "And I've let you forget for too long how much I care."

"You just miss the porn star level sex," Remy said, hiding his surprise and longing behind humor.

Aden let out a loud whimper. "Aye. So much. Mostly, though, I miss this—being with you. I miss my friend."

In the face of Aden's confession, Remy found himself making one. "I miss happiness. When you flew off to Dublin and tried killing yourself, that's what you really killed that day. I haven't been happy since." Thankfully, the hotel came into view, saving Remy from baring any more of his heart. As things stood, he'd already have to be over-the-top obnoxious for the rest of Aden's visit just to save his pride.

"How long did you say you're in town?"

"I didn't."

Fantastic. Split-personalityville here Remy came.

Chapter 4

The moment they were inside Remy's penthouse, Remy pointed Aden in the direction of a spare bedroom and disappeared inside his. Since Aden couldn't breathe, he couldn't argue. He'd known, when he'd flown home determined to end his life, he'd been taking the easy way out. It wasn't a cry for help or attention. For Aden, he'd been done with this life. In his screwed-up state of mind, he'd honestly believed he would be setting Remy free of the burden of him. He'd never been angrier in his life than he'd been when he'd woken up in that hospital still breathing. It might not have made sense to anyone else, but his failed attempt felt like another way he'd let Remy down. Since then, Aden had too many reasons to hate himself to count. He hadn't considered how trying to kill himself had affected Remy. Aden had assumed his night with Boston had slaughtered any and all love Remy had for him.

Their bedrooms were next to each other. He could hear Remy moving around next door. The desire to kick down the door and demand Remy take back his words and promise to be happy was crippling. Aden paced the floor, wanting to tear off his skin. The look on Remy's face, after that douche at the gym had torn him down, sat in Aden's gut. God, he missed getting high and not caring. Aden's feet froze to the floor at the thought. That was how Remy had looked—exactly like Aden had felt every second of every day until finally turning to drugs for relief.

This place; it was bad. There was too much pressure to be perfect and on top. The sound of the shower firing to life cut through Aden's thoughts. He moved to the bathroom inside his room. Remy's shower sounded ridiculously loud through the wall. The man he loved was right there—nude and just out of sight. Aden turned the knob, switching on his shower. He peeled off his clothes as steam filled the bathroom. The memory slammed into him without mercy.

Beads of hot water trailed down Remy's spine before caressing the curve of his ass. Aden's mouth watered at the sight. He imagined the flavor of each drop. Anything that had touched Remy's skin had to taste like the most expensive single malt. Without thought, Aden dropped to his knees and captured the beads on his tongue. He'd been right. They tasted amazing, but only made him want more. His teeth sank into Remy's ass

71

cheek. The moan filling the shower had Aden's dick leaking. He never got enough of Remy. Aden bit the man again because he needed Remy's moans like oxygen. Remy's palms flattened on the shower wall, as if his knees weren't enough to hold him.

Chill bumps formed on Remy's skin as Aden's teeth scraped the man's ass cheek. Oh, God. He loved that shit. Water sloshed over his hands as Aden swept them up Remy's thighs, moving toward his prize. He knew Remy was hard for him, but he needed to feel the man's erection sliding across his palm.

"Aden." The whisper of his name sounded like cannon fire to Aden's over-sensitized senses.

Aden encircled Remy's cock before responding. "My heart." His words sounded so guttural, they were close to demonic. He could scarcely breathe around his lust. His lips found the small of Remy's back.

Remy sucked in a hiss. "What are you doing to me?"

"Worshipping you," Aden answered without hesitation. If he could go without food or sleep, Aden would do this nonstop. Remy was that big of an infatuation for Aden. He urged Remy's hips back, half wondering if he could drown like this. It would be the best way to go,

bringing his man pleasure. Shifting positions, Aden spread Remy's cheeks wide, exposing his gorgeous asshole. Remy was panting. It was music to Aden's ears. He tongued the man's hole, letting the noises Remy made guide him. Aden's dick knew he was only minutes away from fucking this man who rocked his world. It twitched with joy and anticipation.

"Fuck me, Aden. Quit teasing."

Tilting his head back, Aden let the hot water scald his face, hoping to wash away the memory. He'd never have those days back. The knowledge didn't stop him from fucking his fist like it was Remy's tight ass. Aden hadn't been lying. Being with Remy went beyond the porn star level the man claimed. He'd ruined Aden for anyone else. More than anything, Aden missed the words Remy whispered against his skin as Aden buried himself inside Remy's body. Praise. Love. Ridiculous stories about forever. It was all gone. Poised on the edge of orgasm, Aden froze, accepting his body's screams of protest. He didn't deserve to think of Remy as he orgasmed. Since he couldn't stop thinking about Remy, there'd be no pleasure for him. Self-hatred lay down that path. Instead, Aden bit the inside of his cheek until he tasted blood, and washed his hair.

*

Lukewarm water washed over Remy's skin. It had started out scalding. He'd stood under the stream with his forehead pressed against the shower wall for so long, cold water threatened to overtake him. He was cool with that. His body had gone numb the instant he'd heard Aden's shower fire to life just on the other side of this wall. If he had a sledgehammer, they'd already be together. Thankfully, he didn't and was saved from ruin.

Remy wasn't completely insane. He recognized what he really wanted was the past. If he owned a giant eraser, one that could wipe away every mistake standing between them, Remy would tear down this wall. Otherwise, there was nothing but pain and loss. The problem was—since seeing Aden again—he didn't feel it anymore. The love was back, eating away at his brain. Now all he knew was sheer fucking terror. Aden would never understand what it had been like for him—getting that call. The one saying Aden wasn't expected to live. The fury; it had been bigger than anything he'd ever faced. Aden had fucked everything they were and then tried leaving this world permanently. The man had been halfway around the world, clinging to life, and Remy wanted to kill him for it.

Now he just felt... robbed—of his life, his anger, but most of all, of the happily-ever-after he was supposed to get with Aden. At some point, one even Remy couldn't define, the pain had broken him.

Remy shut down the water because he couldn't stand himself a second longer. Because he was an ass, Remy moved like a sloth through his routine of getting ready for a night on the town. The end result was pretty fucking fantastic, if Remy said so himself. He went in search of Aden. When Remy found him, his heart dropped to his stomach. He realized the truth. Looking like a billion bucks might've won Remy the battle, but Aden won the war.

Asleep on his stomach and wearing nothing more than his boxer briefs, Aden was the definition of temptation. Aden's entire adult life had been spent inside a gym. His body showed it in every line. He was a hard mountain with deep valleys. Remy wanted to lick every inch. His lips went numb with desire. He forced his feet to stay put right inside the bedroom doorway, ensuring he wouldn't accidentally pounce.

"You really are getting old if I've worn you out already."

Aden's head popped up at Remy's statement. His face was sleep-swollen and his hair stood on end. Remy bit his bottom lip to keep from smiling. Aden rolled onto his back, giving Remy an eyeful of impressive package. He was thankful he'd already been biting his lip. It kept his moan from slipping out.

Aden scrubbed his hands over his face. "Sorry about that."

Remy shook his head. "It's my fault. I forgot about the time difference. It's later for you. Plus, you've had a big day."

As if realizing he was near to being nude, Aden snagged his jeans and sat up. "Love the shoes," Aden said as he came to his feet and shoved one leg inside his jeans.

Remy dropped his gaze to the silver sneakers that sparkled when the light hit them just right. "Shiny things make me happy," Remy said, glancing back up in time to catch him doing the jeans shimmy. All those squats made jeans almost impossible to wear. He had to pry them over his massive thighs, but then they were too big in the waist. They sagged, showing off the sexy obliques. Seriously, Remy didn't stand a chance. He nearly whimpered as Aden pulled a black T-shirt on,

76

covering up his abs. It wasn't fair. Remy had spent over an hour getting ready, trying for perfection. Aden woke up, tossed on some clothes, and *voila*—sexy god.

"You never said what we're doing," Aden said, reminding Remy to get his head back in the game.

"This is Vegas. The world is our oyster."

Aden scowled.

Remy chuckled. "Seriously, how many times have you been here?"

"For matches? Hundreds."

"But how many nights on the town have you enjoyed?" Remy asked.

"I don't find its wares enjoyable."

Remy smoothed his hands down his shirt. "That was before I became part of the wares," Remy reminded him.

"Was that an offer to partake?" Aden asked, his voice sounding husky.

Without thought, Remy winked. "Nope. I'm also not taking you on the town," he said with a laugh. "There's a casino downstairs. We're going gambling."

"All right," Aden said, stomping into a worn out looking pair of work boots without tying them.

Remy shook his head as he took in the full picture. Aden's black tight-fit V-neck T-shirt strained against the muscles in Aden's chest and arms. The legs of his jeans balled up at the tops of the work boots that had seen some stuff—probably the eighties. The man obviously had no intention of brushing his hair. Damned if Aden wasn't the hottest man Remy had ever seen.

"What?" Aden asked—clueless.

Since "I want to fuck you" wasn't a reasonable answer given the current climate, Remy shook his head again. "Nothing."

Without warning, Aden snagged Remy by the back of the neck and claimed his mouth. The kiss was hard and hot. It was searching and finding all Remy's hottest fantasies. By the time Aden pulled away, Remy was struggling for air and gripping Aden's shirt like he'd melt to the floor without it.

"Do you remember yet?"

Remy blinked, not understanding the question. "What?"

It was Aden's turn to shake his head. "Nothing." When he stepped back, disappointment washed over Remy, nearly knocking him off his feet. He needed to hear Aden's thoughts. Whatever he wanted Remy to remember, Remy wanted it too. Since Aden was headed for the door, Remy had no other choice but to let it go for now.

* * *

Remy blew a hundred dollars on slots in a matter of minutes. He didn't care. It was all in fun, and truly, he wanted to get back to being with Aden, who'd chosen a different level of slots. Remy never went higher than the penny machines. Aden had plopped down at the first quarter machine he came to and hadn't budged. With his limit met on spending for the night, Remy claimed the empty seat next to Aden, pulling it as close to Aden's side as possible before sitting.

"That was fun."

Aden glanced over. "Done already?"

Remy shrugged. "It's more fun to watch anyhow. How's it going?"

"Losing my arse," Aden said on a chuckle. He glanced over as he made the claim and his eyes shone with good humor. The green irises were so fucking gorgeous, Remy forgot where they were for a moment.

"Never fear, I'm here now. I'm your lucky charm, remember?"

"That you are," Aden agreed without missing a beat.

Aden lost another dollar.

Reaching over, Remy touched the screen with the tip of his finger. "There you go. You'll win now."

The pressure of Aden's thigh increased against Remy's leg. Remy dropped his gaze. Aden's arm rested on his thigh. Without thought, Remy set his fingers on Aden's forearm. Aden immediately turned his arm over, palm up, as if waiting for Remy to take his hand. Remy's gaze locked on the deep and jagged scar running from Aden's palm to the bend of his arm. His throat swelled as he automatically traced the line with his fingertips before linking his fingers through Aden's. When he looked back up, Aden was watching him. Neither of them said a word. Sometimes, there weren't any. Other times, there were too many. Remy wasn't sure any longer which case applied to them. He'd gotten by believing he had nothing left to say to this man who'd destroyed him. Now, with their palms pressed together, he wasn't so sure.

"Remy—"

Remy looked away. "You're winning." Even to him, his voice sounded broken.

Aden glanced at the screen. "What the feck? How did that happen?" Aden was five hundred dollars up.

"Cash out before you start losing again."

Aden hit the button to print off the receipt for his winnings. "I'm thinking I should give this to you, since I was losing before you came along."

"Keep it," Remy said, coming to his feet. "You'll need it to buy me dinner at the crazy-expensive buffet they have here."

"You're on."

After finding a machine, and cashing out his ticket, they hit the restaurant. Remy picked at his food while listening to Aden tell a story about a brutal interview he'd sat through with Daniel Long before coming to Vegas.

"He'll probably eat me alive when it releases," Aden finished with a flourish. "That little bastard has never liked me."

A smile tugged at the corners of Remy's mouth. "Probably because you always refer to him as a 'little bastard.'"

Aden shrugged. "There's that. Mostly, though, it's because he's always had his eye on you, but you ignore him."

Remy huffed. "You're always thinking people have their eye on me when they don't. I'm a unique flavor. Just because it's one you love doesn't mean everyone does."

He swore Aden's eyes darkened. "Aye. I do love you." He smiled, taking away the heaviness of his statement. "But, in this case, one has nothing to do with the other. It's not hard to spot people's lustful stares. I know that look well. It's the way I've been looking at you since you moonwalked into my life. And you're not wearing your eyeliner again. What's up with that?"

Remy fiddled with the napkin next to his plate. "I told you, people don't accept me here."

Aden looked around at the freak show happening around them. "Are you feckin' kidding me?"

"It's hard to explain," Remy said, feeling defensive.

"To the pope, maybe," Aden argued. "But you're talking to me."

Remy shrugged. "When I'm alone or have only a few small errands to run, I'm okay to be me. If I'm at No Rival for the day or out for the night, I don't like rocking the boat. I don't want to make people stare any more than they already do."

The way Aden shook his head, as if disappointed, made the muscles in Remy's stomach clench. "It's a damn good thing I showed up, then," Aden said, tossing some money on the table for a tip. "Let's go."

Since Aden was using his "I'm in charge here" tone, Remy knew the rest of the night was out of his hands. "Where are we going?"

"To put a stop to this bullshit. I want *my* Remy back."

Remy tried to work up an ounce of guilt over the trill of excitement running through him. He shouldn't be this happy about anything to do with Aden. Yet he couldn't stop smiling as he followed in Aden's long stride toward the concierge desk. Aden spoke to the man working in quiet tones, refusing to let Remy take part. With whatever information he sought acquired, Aden snagged Remy's hand and headed for the door.

"Should I grab my car keys?"

Aden tossed a wink Remy's way. "Nope. You're not hiding in your car and you're not hiding me. Everything we need is within walking distance and you'll hold my hand on the way there. Understood?"

Remy tried for a solemn nod, but his stupid grin wouldn't abate. He'd missed the way Aden took over his life, making everything okay. For two blocks, Remy held Aden's hand and the pride... fuck. He'd forgotten how proud he'd been when this man was his. When they were training, Remy teased and flirted, but he'd kept their secret, because he didn't want Aden to get in trouble. Outside the gym, when they'd gone out of town for competitions, this had been their life. People stared, but not because they expected Remy would do something stupid. Aden was that goddamn sexy. He walked like a man you wanted to watch walk. He had swagger. His head was always held high and his shoulders thrown back. The way his hips moved... wow.

As quickly as the pride hit, so too did the memories. When he'd learned about Aden's night with Boston, Remy had felt like all these proud moments were lies.

Every time he'd felt special, because Aden wanted him above all others—bullshit. That had been anger and pain talking; now he remembered it all. Aden was an amazing person. Before he could change his mind, Remy pulled Aden to a stop. When Aden looked over, eyebrows raised in question, Remy let the confession fly before he changed his mind.

"I didn't sleep with Boston. Gunnar didn't see what he thought he saw."

The dimple below Aden's eye made an appearance. "I know. I never doubted you."

Remy didn't miss the truth resonating in Aden's voice. He honestly hadn't believed Remy capable of sleeping with Boston behind Gunnar's back. Remy gave a sharp nod. "Okay, then." Even though he didn't know why, it felt like a win.

*

When they reached the department store, the concierge had suggested, Remy looked at Aden with open curiosity. Aden didn't give in. As they neared the cosmetics counter, Remy's steps slowed. Aden dug in his heels, refusing to slow. A woman wearing a black smock smiled brightly at their approach.

"Can I help you find something?"

Aden nodded and pulled Remy past him before shoving him toward the woman. "My heart needs a makeover to brighten his day."

Proving the man at the hotel had deserved the big tip Aden had given him for his services, the woman clapped her hands and bounced in place. Her excitement was catching as she eyed Remy. "Fantastic. Between your gorgeous eyes and bone structure, I cannot wait. Do you have any thoughts on what you'd like?"

Remy's expression was priceless. "Um…"

Aden found an empty chair and planted his ass, expecting a long wait. "He needs something bright and flashy to match his wild heart."

"I don't want to look like a two-dollar whore," Remy said, sounding horrified and making Aden laugh.

The woman urged Remy to sit on the empty stool by the counter but looked to Aden in answer. "I think you're the one with the best ideas here. What do you think?"

Aden shrugged. "I don't care. My only job is to mess it up later," he said, not bothering to keep the sexual tint from his voice.

Her musical laughter let him know she wasn't bothered. She glanced Remy's way and snorted. "I see I won't need to use any blush. You have that covered."

Remy was blushing. It was hot. The woman got started and Aden tuned everything out. Remy's confession kept snaking its way into his brain, eating away at him. He'd always known in his heart Remy hadn't slept with Boston. Like he'd told Gunnar, he didn't know what Gunnar had walked in on that day, but it wasn't sexual.

Aden's gaze landed on a set of stencils. He tried to think of some reason for their existence and came up empty. There was a snowflake, cloud, and sun—like something a child would use for coloring. Aden couldn't tear his gaze away. A smile touched his lips as he realized why.

"Are you covered in chalk?"

Remy's eyes skirted away. Guilt etched his features—like a kid who'd gotten caught eating candy before dinner. "Possibly."

A snort escaped Aden. "Ain't no possibly about it. The tip of your nose is blue."

Remy swiped at his nose, making it worse. He glanced down at his hands. Aden dropped his gaze as well. Remy's hands were covered in a rainbow of colors.

"You may as well spill."

Remy shifted his weight from foot to foot, looking uncomfortable. "Well, you remember how you said you wanted to paint the bedroom?"

A bad feeling rose in Aden's gut. "Aye."

"You may want to do it sooner rather than later."

Aden's gaze shot to the closed bedroom door. He stepped around Remy. His long stride ate up the floor. He expected anything. He was still unprepared for the inside of his room. Every inch of bare wall was covered in chalk drawings—like a kid on crack had been set loose in his bedroom with sidewalk chalk. Giant hearts and rainbows assailed his senses, as well as a bright yellow sun drawn in one of the upper corners. It was like the inside of Remy's unicorn mind had exploded on his bedroom walls. Flipping his eyes to the ceiling, Aden tried to decide how to react. Huge bubbly letters on the ceiling caught Aden's attention.

"Happy birthday, Aden. I love you."

Aden blinked at the message. Neither of them had said the words, but Aden definitely felt them. The backs of his eyes burned and his throat swelled.

"Now I don't want to paint in here. It's gorgeous."

Aden motioned toward the stencils. "What are these for?"

The saleswoman flashed Aden a wicked grin. "Great call. Which one do you like?"

"The sun," Aden answered without hesitation. "Remy brightens everyone's day—like the sun."

"Awww. That's sweet," the woman cooed as she held the stencil to the apple of Remy's cheek. "See, you use a little pearl coloring," she said, tracing the tiny sun on Remy's face. "And it's pretty much invisible until the light hits it." She tilted Remy's chin until light hit the mark at just the right angle, making the sun sparkle. It was perfect.

"You're about to get a huge tip. Just so you know," Aden said, letting the woman know how much he liked her work.

"It's been fun," she said, sounding unconcerned.

"So you're finished, then?"

She nodded. "Remy doesn't need much, since he's a natural beauty."

Aden winked. "He doesn't need anything at all, but pretty things make him smile, and that makes me happy."

"You're doing a lot of talking about me like I'm not sitting here."

Aden met Remy's painted stare. His steel blue eyes stood out beautifully in contrast to the dark shading surrounding them. "Am I wrong?"

Remy smiled but didn't respond. Instead, he focused on the saleswoman. "I want to buy the eyeshadow."

While Remy was distracted with making his purchase, Aden set the second half of his plan into action. After leaving the woman the huge tip he'd promised, Aden reclaimed Remy's hand and headed for the door. Before they stepped out of the store's light, Aden pulled Remy to a stop. Snagging the man's chin, Aden inspected the woman's work. The light hit the sun on Remy's cheek, pulling a smile from Aden.

"Very nice." He met Remy's gaze. If Remy was

happy with his new look, he didn't show it. His expression remained clear of all emotion as he held Aden's stare. Aden couldn't take not knowing. "Do you like it?"

"She did a good job," Remy said, not really answering the question.

Aden couldn't hide his disappointment. "I'd hoped when you showed up twice at my gym, wearing eyeliner, you were finally living as openly in public as you'd done in private with me when we were together. But don't worry. I won't put you on display since I see that isn't the case. For the record, I hate that you're hiding," Aden said before stepping away. As much as he wanted to kiss Remy and hold his hand, he'd just given his word he wouldn't. Remy followed silently on Aden's heels as he headed outside. The limo he'd called already sat at the curb, waiting. The driver held open the door. Aden waved Remy in ahead of him before climbing in behind him.

The instant the door closed behind them, Remy's voice cut through the darkness, sounding hollow. "Where are we going?"

Aden shook his head and raised the partition to give them privacy. "Nowhere. I told them I wanted to see the city. So they're driving us around for the next hour. I told you I wasn't trying to put you on display. You're with me. I just want to be with you."

Without a word, Remy moved forward and climbed into Aden's lap. Aden's heart swelled as Remy settled against him, fitting perfectly in his arms. "I'm not hiding," Remy said, sounding certain. "I don't match."

Aden snorted at the asinine comment. "You just said she did a good job."

Remy shook his head. Aden felt it more than saw it happen. "My outside doesn't match my inside anymore." Before Aden could puzzle that one out, Remy changed the subject. "An hour is a long time for sightseeing."

Aden's arms tightened around Remy and he spoke against the man's ear. "Not when I'm with you. It's the blink of an eye." Aden's lips moved to Remy's cheek, finding the sun drawn there. Softly, he hummed the song about Remy being his sunshine until he felt the man's cheek curve into a smile.

"I didn't want to remember this side of you," Remy whispered into the dark, as if it was the deepest confession. It triggered Aden's admission.

"I don't ever want to forget anything about you."

Aden tried holding Remy closer. "After your match this weekend, I'll go home. You never have to see me again."

"Tell the driver to take us back to the hotel."

Aden's heart fell at Remy's demand, but he hit the intercom button and did as asked. He'd known winning Remy back would be a longshot, if not impossible. Knowing didn't ease the pain. Remy didn't move from his lap. Aden took what he could.

"You told Emily you would mess up my makeup."

"Who is Emily?"

Remy shook with barely suppressed laughter. "The lady from the cosmetics counter. You told her it was your job to mess it up. I don't like it when you don't keep your word."

Aden held his breath to steady his voice. He didn't want to misunderstand. "I don't want you to think I only came here for that. As I said earlier, I've missed my friend."

Remy nodded. "So you don't intend to keep your word?"

"I didn't bring any protection with me," Aden said, putting it out there and hoping Remy didn't punch him

93

in the dick for assuming.

"Don't worry," Remy said softly as he shifted positions in Aden's lap. "You can trust me to take care of you." Remy's lips found his and Aden melted into his touch, immediately opening. His mind and body went to war. The soft brush of tongue on tongue tugged at Aden's heartstrings, making him long for the nights of slow lovemaking. The nights when they'd kissed and caressed all night. His raging and overly neglected hard-on screamed for Aden to fuck Remy hard and fast before he lost the chance.

When the car came to stop and Remy pulled away, taking his love with him, Aden's muscles tensed. He fought the urge to jump from the car and race back to the room. Instead, he waited with a patience he didn't feel for the driver to set them free. Aden measured every movement as he passed some money the driver's way before claiming Remy's hand and heading for the elevator. He didn't look left or right. Neither did he hurry. Instead, he took his time, while grinding his back teeth to a pulp. Once the elevator door slid closed, Aden chanced a glance Remy's way. His face was turned away, but the curve of his cheek let Aden know Remy was smiling. The tension in his shoulders eased.

He brushed his fingers down the back of Remy's neck, bringing the man's attention his way. When his sexy eyes focused on Aden, Aden automatically moved closer.

"You're beautiful." He could tell Remy was holding his breath, waiting for more. Aden let him have it. "I want to strip you out of these clothes and taste every inch of your skin. The way you quiver against my tongue." Aden sucked in a deep breath. "That shit gets me so feckin' high."

Remy's gaze dropped to Aden's mouth.

Aden smirked. "Aye. You remember what I can do for you."

Remy visibly shivered at the claim.

Aden nearly came in his jeans right then. He also hadn't forgotten a single detail. Remy was the most responsive sexual person Aden had ever met. He didn't hold back. He cupped Remy's jaw and dragged his thumb down Remy's bottom lip, picturing his teeth sinking into its plump deliciousness. Remy's eyes glazed over, making Aden's dick even harder.

"I wonder if I hit the emergency stop button and dropped to my knees, if I could suck you off before help

95

arrived."

Remy whimpered.

Aden's hand shot out. "Let's find out."

Remy jumped like someone had lit a fire under his ass, reaching for Aden's arm. "No," he cried as he snagged Aden's hand before he could press the button. Not that Aden had intended to really push it.

Aden used Remy's momentum against him, pulling the man against his chest and burying his face against his throat. "Now I have you," Aden said, growling the words against Remy's skin. The elevator door slid open, and they spilled out into Remy's penthouse. Instead of immediately sweeping Remy off his feet, Aden not-so-patiently watched as Remy turned the key in the control panel, stopping the elevator from opening on this floor for anyone else for the night.

Aden peeled his shirt off as he waited. The moment Remy finished his task, Aden snatched the man off his feet and tossed him over his shoulder. Remy's laughter filled the penthouse as Aden headed for Remy's bedroom. Aden barely spared a glance for the room as he crossed the threshold into Remy's personal space, although he couldn't help but note it seemed somewhat impersonal for a place Remy had been living for a few years. At the moment, he didn't have enough blood reaching his brain to work things out. He had a sexy man over his shoulder. Priorities.

The instant he cleared the bedroom, Aden set Remy on his feet. He let the man slide down his body. His breath caught as Remy's shirt slid upward as Remy got closer to the floor. Their bare torsos pressed against each other. Aden moved slow, refusing to let go of Remy. He held Remy's stare. They were connected on a deeper level than most. Aden had always known it. Feckin' hell. He'd missed this. No one looked at Aden the way Remy did.

The man's lips were slightly parted—anticipating. After snagging the hem of Remy's shirt, Aden dragged the material over Remy's head. He tossed the shirt aside. He didn't care where it landed. All Aden cared about was the way Remy's body felt against his.

"I want to kiss you, but I'm afraid to close my eyes."

Remy's expression turned to longing. "Why?"

"You might disappear," Aden admitted, uncaring if his fears sounded ridiculous. Remy had already disappeared from his life once. He'd wanted to die then too.

"Then kiss me with your eyes open," Remy said, making everything seem so simple. Aden flattened his palms on Remy's bare back, savoring having Remy in his arms. The air stuttered in Aden's throat, sounding unnaturally loud.

Moving slow, Aden dipped his head and touched his lips to the corner of Remy's mouth. "Do you remember?" Aden asked as he moved to Remy's ear.

Remy shoved his hands down the back of Aden's jeans, clawing at his skin and trying to pull Aden closer. "That's the second time you've asked me that," Remy said, sounding breathless. "You keep my brain too fogged to read your mind."

Aden popped the button loose on Remy's pants and slid his zipper down. "Tell your brain to shove off," Aden said as his lips moved to Remy's collarbone. "I'm talking to your body right now." Aden brushed Remy's skin with his lips, doing just that—whispering to the man's body. "Do you feel my love? Do you remember how much and hard I loved you—still love you?" Aden shoved Remy's pants down, revealing the sexy curve of the man's ass. "Can you feel my heart racing, trying to beat through my chest to find its owner? I don't want you to think with your head. Your head still hates me a little. The rest of you remembers us," Aden said as he fell to his knees and pressed his face to Remy's stomach. "Everything is the same," Aden said. Hot tears threatened to push through, but no way was that happening. He peeled Remy's pants and underwear down his legs, not stopping until Remy stood completely nude. "I've never let you go," Aden swore before swallowing Remy's cock. He felt Remy sway on his feet. Aden snagged the man's hips, holding him in place and prepared to catch him if he lost the battle with his knees.

He sucked hard, trying to savor the moment. Remy might be small in build, but he had a huge dick and Aden had always loved taking the whole thing down his throat. The way Remy moaned and begged made Aden feel as if Remy belonged to him again—if only in body. He rolled Remy's balls between his fingers before urging his thighs apart and massaging his asshole. The mewling sounds falling from Remy's perfect lips had Aden giving it everything he had. He licked, sucked, and swirled his tongue around Remy's crown. Aden hummed his enjoyment of the man's flavor as Remy's pre-cum smeared across his tongue. The pressure of his jeans, squashing his erection, had Aden coming to his feet. Remy whimpered in protest but held on to Aden's neck when Aden swept the man into his arms. He sought Remy's lips before heading for the bed. Aden forced himself to keep their kiss short. He could kiss

Remy for the rest of his life, but then he'd miss out on the rest. In a show of his love, because he was ruled by it with Remy, Aden gently set Remy on the bed before stripping off his jeans and joining Remy. Starting at the end of the bed, Aden crawled on and grabbed Remy's ankle. "I hope you're ready for a long night, because I am." He felt Remy shiver and an evil grin pulled at his lips. Yeah. Remy hadn't answered any of his questions, but the man knew the truth. He knew Aden loved him and what it was like when Aden made love to him.

*

Remy swallowed down a cry when Aden's lips touched his ankle. He recognized the man's expression. Aden intended to drag out Remy's pleasure until he begged for Aden's mercy. The aggressive blowjob he'd gotten only moments earlier had merely been a preview of things to come. With Aden, Remy knew he wouldn't get the final show until Aden quenched his sensual cravings, and Aden was a sensual glutton. Aden's lips moved from Remy's ankle and up his calf until he reached Remy's knee. Remy wondered if his heart would explode inside his chest. His dick leaked onto his stomach and his fingers tore at the blankets to keep from scratching at Aden's skin. He knew the harder he fought to force Aden into giving him what he wanted, the slower Aden would move. The man was cruel like that.

By the time Aden's tongue brushed Remy's hipbone, Remy was nothing more than one giant nerve, ready to burst. Aden's eyes flickered upward. Remy stopped breathing at their heat. He couldn't blink or look away. The intensity of the moment kept him frozen. While holding Remy's gaze, Aden slowly lowered his head and dragged his tongue up Remy's erection before taking Remy's crown between his lips.

"Aden." The gasp of Aden's name sounded like a gunshot ricocheting off the walls of Remy's bedroom. As if the sound of his name drove Aden, he swallowed Remy's dick, taking him to the back of his throat before sucking—hard. Remy was lost to the pleasure Aden created. A jumble of words escaped Remy—praise and god only knew what else. He no longer cared as long as Aden didn't stop. It was more than the sensation of Aden's hot mouth tugging at his dick. For Remy, it was the entire package. The way Aden's shoulders moved as he tried caressing every inch of Remy. The sounds he made around Remy's cock. Everything. He never wanted the night to end. There was no stopping time or his rising orgasm. The pressure curling his toes and tightening his balls crawled up his erection and beat at his crown. Every muscle in Remy's body tensed in anticipation of release. Remy's fingers found Aden's hair and held on as he openly took his pleasure. When Remy's orgasm hit, the world tilted. He no longer knew where he stood with Aden. It was like they were back in New Orleans at the height of their love.

Aden swiped his face across Remy's stomach, wiping away the moisture before coming up onto his knees. "Where are those condoms?"

Remy motioned toward the side table. Aden was in the drawer and suited up before Remy knew what happened. Aden's tongue filled Remy's mouth. He overwhelmed Remy even as pushed Remy's knees higher. As he pushed his way inside Remy's ass, Remy sucked in a deep breath against the intrusion. He'd forgotten how damn big Aden was. There were a thousand things he'd forgotten. Aden never danced, but Remy knew he could. The way the man gyrated against him while staying deep reminded Remy of the way a stripper moved. That was the last clear thought Remy had as his body's demands took precedence.

Everything about Aden was rough and raw. Remy felt consumed and commanded. He also felt free. For so long now, he'd been in tight control, never allowing anyone to help him let go or sneak past his walls. Aden had taken over again, leaving Remy free to enjoy the moment and let everything go. He kissed Aden deep, never wanting to stop. Any time Aden pulled back for a moment, Remy drew him back in, needing the man's mouth meshing with his.

When Aden came, his breath caught at the back of his throat in a gasp. Remy felt it against his tongue. Remy scratched at Aden's back, trying to pull him closer. Hold him tighter. If their moment was over, Remy didn't want to feel it happen. Aden rocked against him slowly, riding out the last waves. When Aden rolled to his back, Remy went with him, draping over the man's chest like a blanket. Aden's heart raced beneath Remy's ear. Remy pressed closer. He'd missed that sound. He didn't know how long he listened. All he knew was he couldn't move away. For the first time in forever, he didn't feel alone.

Aden stirred beneath him, making Remy realize he was still awake. "You should be exhausted. I could scoot over if I'm keeping you awake."

Aden's arms tightened around him, threating to squeeze the air from Remy's lungs. "Feck that. It's not you. I'm scared to fall asleep."

Remy shifted, setting his chin on Aden's chest and

meeting the man's gaze. "What's wrong?"

For a second, Aden chewed his bottom lip before giving in and answering. "What if all this is just a dream? What if I wake up to find you gone and all this was in my head?"

Without giving any thought to his actions, Remy pinched Aden's side—hard.

"Ow. What the bloody hell?"

Remy couldn't stop the smile from spreading across his face. "You feel real enough to me."

Aden pinched Remy's ass, getting his revenge. He immediately smoothed his hand over the spot he'd pinched in silent apology. "Kiss me."

He didn't have to think about it. Remy climbed Aden's body and captured the man's lips. If Aden didn't want to sleep, Remy could find the man something else to do. He knew all about waking up with the memory of a dream lost, crushing his soul. Remy wouldn't let that happen to Aden. Maybe he'd missed his shot at keeping his man safe when Aden had his meltdown, but it wouldn't happen again.

Chapter 5

The bed was empty. Aden's initial burst of disappointment melted away when he caught sight of the clock. He'd slept later than he'd done in ages. With only a few short days until Remy's title bout, he couldn't hang around all day waiting for Aden to get up and moving. The second thing Aden's gaze landed upon had Aden's mouth pulling into a bright smile. There was a photo of Remy's face taped to the pillow. His eyes were closed as if he was still sleeping next to Aden. Aden couldn't hold back his laughter. He hopped from the bed, needing to get to No Rival so he could see the real thing again.

In the bathroom, Aden's steps faltered, and a chuckle escaped him. A picture of Remy brushing his teeth was taped to the mirror above the sink. Aden couldn't stop staring at the picture while he brushed his teeth. His cheeks ached from the happiness. God, he'd missed all of Remy's hijinks. Throughout the apartment, Aden stumbled across several more pictures of Remy doing mundane things. Aden left them where he found them and went in search of more. At the dining room table, he found a plate of food waiting for him and another image. This time, Remy's face sat perched against the chair opposite of Aden's food. Aden sat and enjoyed his muffins and fruit while staring at an image of Remy eating a banana. Underneath Remy's face, Remy had scrawled Aden a note in Sharpie. "Paper Pete made you breakfast." Aden snorted for the third time as he re-read the note. Jesus, his life had been so empty without Remy.

He considered jogging to No Rival, so he could run back with Remy at the end of the day. In the end, the need to see Remy as quickly as possible won out. As he punched the code in to get inside No Rival, he wondered if Drew would kick him back out again. It wasn't as if he had any right to be there beyond the man's good graces. When he cleared the doorway, he spotted Drew sitting behind his desk. He glanced up at Aden's arrival.

"Aden," Drew called out, stopping Aden before he could go in search of Remy. "Can I talk to you for a minute before you take over my training schedule for the day?"

Aden flushed as he moved to join Drew. "Sorry if I'm overstepping. Training men to win is in my blood."

Drew waved off Aden's apology. "Actually, I was being serious. If you plan to hang around, I'll put you to work."

In his surprise, Aden dipped his chin, unsure if Drew was testing him. "I'm all right with it if you are. After all, it's not as if I'm paying to be here like everyone else. I may as well earn my keep for the next few days while I'm here, working with Remy."

"Don't worry over Remy," Drew said, clearing off his desk and not meeting Aden's gaze. "He's paired with Rhys today. They're—unfortunately—very well matched in personality. I think they'll do great together."

"Rhys?" Aden mused. "You don't mean Rhys Collier, do you?"

"The very one," Drew answered absently, still shifting through the paperwork on his desk as if searching for something. "Actually, it's Rhys D' Ettore now, but it's the same person." Damn. Rhys was the MMA world light heavyweight champion. That was an amazing opportunity for Remy if Rhys didn't kill him. As if reading his mind, Drew finally focused on Aden. "Don't worry. Rhys is like a gigantic obnoxious puppy. Remy will be fine. Anyhow," Drew continued, moving on. "I've already talked to Remy this morning, but I wanted to talk you too and apologize about yesterday. If I'd known Carter harbored so much jealousy toward Remy, I would've intervened sooner. Hopefully, after our talk this morning, Remy will come to me in the future if there's another problem."

Aden snorted. "Not bloody likely. Remy would find a warm pile of shit to sleep in if he could avoid complaining about being cold." As the words left Aden's mouth, a million questions raced through his mind. It was the truth. Remy never complained about a goddamn thing. Had being with Aden been Remy's warm pile of shit? After all, Aden had been a junkie. Being with him couldn't have been an easy life for Remy. How had the man loved Aden at all?

"Well," Drew said, pulling Aden's thoughts away from those dark times. "Even if Remy won't come to me, maybe he now knows I care. I might have my hands full here, but these guys mean the world to me."

Aden didn't doubt it. Drew seemed like a great guy. "I'll mention it to him as well. It might not make any difference, but I can try."

"I'd appreciate it. It's obvious he trusts you above everyone else. The way he immediately mimicked every move you showed him yesterday said a lot about the amount of time you've worked together. I'd hate to break up a pair," Drew said with a laugh. "Get going. I can see I'm killing you, making you sit here with me."

Aden flashed the man a grateful smile. "When you get a minute, just point me in the direction of where I'm needed and I'll jump in."

"Don't worry," Drew said as Aden headed for the door. "You'll get ambushed with requests the moment you step out my office."

With a shake of his head, Aden headed for the training floor. He'd only been there a few hours yesterday, and he'd shown his ass with Carter. Aden doubted anyone would willingly work with him in this place. Fighters were family. The second Aden turned the corner, he tripped over Carter.

"Do you have a minute?"

Aden blinked in surprise at the man's sudden appearance. "Aye."

"I'd like to apologize for yesterday and explain if you don't mind."

"There's no need, but I see you need to get it off your chest, so I'm listening."

Carter gave a sharp nod as if recognizing Aden's time was precious. "I fought for the lightweight title three nights ago and lost." A bitter smile touched the man's lips. "Years of work for nothing. Remy is a nice person."

"Aye, he is," Aden said, understanding what Carter

wasn't saying. Remy was nice and therefore a soft target. Carter had known he could attack Remy and keep his teeth.

"It won't happen again. I've already given Remy my word."

Aden spent a moment eyeing Carter. The man looked nice and seemed to mean every word. His light blue eyes were latched on to Aden. He looked as if he was holding his breath, waiting for Aden's forgiveness. If Remy could forgive him, then so could Aden. "Would you like some help tightening up your moves?"

A smile exploded across Carter's face, making the man look younger than even Remy. "I'd love that. Thank you."

Aden slapped the man across the back and urged him toward a practice mat. "Don't give up after one loss. I'm the best, and I've got you now." Aden didn't know if it was true, or why he was saying as much, but he hadn't lied when he'd been talking to Drew. Training was in his blood. There was nothing he loved more than making men into winners.

*

Several times throughout the day, Remy expected Aden to come around, if for no other reason than to give a few pointers. Instead, he stayed away. Remy tried not to take it to heart. No doubt, after yesterday's bullshit, he thought he was a distraction. The idea was enough to make Remy want to take back his acceptance of Carter's apology. The only thing stopping him from being the one who instigated a locker room brawl was the fact that Aden spent the whole day working with Carter. Leave it to Aden to diffuse a situation by fixing the root of the problem.

Twenty minutes before time to leave, Aden finally made his way over to Remy. Then he only stopped by long enough to tell Remy he was headed back to the hotel and get Remy's elevator key. Remy tried not to let disappointment gnaw at his gut, but the jog home brought with it a black mood he couldn't shake. To be honest, he was always a hair's breadth away from descending into a dark place inside his head. Even the beads of sweat, rolling down his spine, had him ready to tear off his skin or throw himself in front of a bus. He'd never been more sick of anything in his life than he was of himself. It didn't used to be this way.

Aden wasn't supposed to be there. He'd given the man a key months ago, but Remy hadn't expected Aden to use it today. Aden was supposed to be in L.A. There was nothing for it. Remy would have to brazen things out. Unfortunately, when Remy cleared the door, he lost his nerve. While keeping his head down, Remy made a beeline for the bedroom.

"Hey, darling. Give me a sec," Remy called over his shoulder. He almost made it to safety.

"Whoa. Hold up. Where's my kiss?"

Remy's stomach dropped. His feet froze to the floor. No matter how hard he tried, Remy couldn't draw a full breath. In a matter of seconds, Aden would know everything. Remy would lose him. Why hadn't he been capable of letting go of his ridiculous desire? Aden's palm slid across Remy's nape. Remy wondered if he'd puke. At Aden's urging, Remy slowly turned. When their gazes met, Aden's hand fell away. He'd never seen Aden shocked speechless. Remy was seeing it now. Aden cleared his throat. It was an uncomfortable sound.

"This is new."

Remy swiped his palms down the front of his jeans. "Not really, no."

Aden moved a step closer.

Panic rose in Remy's chest. "I'll go wash it off."

To Remy's surprise, Aden shook his head and shifted even closer. He cupped Remy's face. His gaze moved over Remy's features, seeing everything Remy had tried to keep hidden. The tightness in his chest eased, but his breaths still came harder. There was no missing the hunger growing in Aden's expression.

"Bloody hell, my heart. Where have you been hiding this side of yourself?"

Remy shrugged as he struggled for an explanation. "I didn't think you'd still want me if you ever saw me like this."

Aden snagged Remy's hand and urged Remy's fingers to shape the erection growing in Aden's jeans. "You know I can't fake this reaction. Damn, sexy. You don't need any of this stuff painting your face, but I'm so feckin' turned on right now. Jesus. You are the most gorgeous and bravest man I've ever met. Will you be mad if I mess this stuff up? I think I need to get inside you quick and give you a reason to keep me. You're so out of my league."

Remy loved this man who filled him to completion. Never in his life had Remy felt more beautiful on the inside.

Remy stared at his reflection in the elevator's glass as he rode to the top floor of the hotel. There were dark circles under his eyes and his hair was plastered to his face. He didn't look like himself any longer. He didn't feel like himself any longer. There was no happiness anymore. The urge to slam his fist into his reflection had Remy popping his neck, trying to ease the tension.

He didn't want to be this person when he saw Aden. When the doors slid open, he spotted Aden immediately. The man was lighting candles around their dinner. Like that, the darkness bearing down on Remy disappeared.

"What have you been doing while I was gone?"

Aden turned at Remy's question. The sheepish grin pulling at Aden's lips melted Remy's heart. "I hope this is okay."

Remy bit his lip, trying to hold back his smile. "What? Being taken care of? I think I can handle it." The cool air chilled the sweat on his skin, reminding him of how nasty he looked. "I need a shower." He eyed the food on the table. "I'll be quick." Before Remy made it five steps, Aden overcame him. Obviously uncaring of how disgusting Remy currently was, he snagged Remy around the waist and captured his lips. It was fast and deep. When he pulled away, Remy's eyes were hazy.

Aden pulled away. "Hurry."

Without needing to be told twice, Remy rushed to the bedroom. After tearing off his clothes, leaving them where they landed, he jumped in the shower without letting the water warm up first. He didn't care. It had been a long time since he'd been excited about anything. Aden was waiting in the other room. Nothing was more exciting than that. Remy took the fastest shower in history before towel drying his hair and throwing on the first clothes he came to. Normally, he'd take his time, ensuring he looked his absolute best, but it was Aden. Aden loved him just as he was—imperfections and all.

He found Aden waiting at the table and staring into space. Remy slipped into the seat across from him. "You didn't have to do all this."

Aden startled, as if he'd been so lost in thought he hadn't noticed Remy's arrival. His smile reappeared. "Yes, I did. How did training go with Rhys?"

It felt like it had been forever since anyone had asked him about his day. He hadn't realized how much he missed having someone to talk to until Aden was there, hanging on every word. Remy set into an explanation of the differences between working Carter and Rhys, not realizing until that moment how much more he'd enjoyed his day. Rhys was a titleholder, just like Remy, even if it was in a different sport. The man had already met his goals in life and wasn't concerned if he ever won again. He was enjoying doing what he loved while spending as much time as possible with his husband and child.

The food was gone and Remy didn't remember taking a bite. All he knew for certain was he'd dominated the conversation. He fell silent, hoping Aden would take over. Aden kept switching his attention between the table and Remy, as if still waiting for Remy's reaction to the candlelight dinner or trying to hide his nerves. The third time Aden looked away, Remy couldn't take it any longer. A laugh escaped him. Aden was so damn adorable when he was nervous.

"What's on your mind, darling?"

Aden's hands shifted from his lap to the table. A thick envelope was clasped between his fingers. Aden eyed the paper in his hands. "I wrote this for you when I was in rehab." A muscle in Remy's chest jumped. He didn't know if his body fought to spring and snatch the letter from Aden's hands or cower. Aden wouldn't look at him. "Several times I thought to send it to you. Then the time limit passed for it to be appropriate to send you anything. I've almost thrown it away a hundred times. Something always stops me. I'm still not sure if giving it to you is the right decision, but—"

Remy snatched the letter from Aden's hands without giving the man time to stop him. Aden finally met his gaze. He looked resigned. Remy almost handed the envelope back. When Aden's hands fell back to his lap, he continued holding Remy's gaze—accepting. Remy jumped to his feet once more. He pressed a quick kiss to Aden's lips before reclaiming his seat.

"It's okay, darling," Remy said, trying to reassure him. Even Remy wasn't sure if it was true, but he needed to know what the letter said. He slipped the note from the envelope and unfolded it. Remy held his breath, prayed for strength, and read what was inside.

Remy, (This letter is dedicated to your eyes.)

Today is day forty-seven without you. I wanted to write to you sooner, but this is the first day they've trusted me with writing utensils. It's odd. I never thought there'd come a time when anyone would believe I'm such a danger to myself I wouldn't be allowed to use a pen. That's a low moment, indeed.

Remy fought the urge to toss the letter aside. He knew Aden watched him. That was the only thing that stopped him from doing just that. He didn't need to know about Aden's time in rehab.

Of course, I also never dreamed I'd hurt you, but here we are.

Remy drew a slow breath in through his nose, trying to squelch the pain.

When I made the decision to write this letter, I'd thought to explain. Now that I'm putting pen to paper, I realize there're no words. There's only me before you and what's left of me after you. You fell in love with a mess. Why did you do that? You were always so much better than me.

In spite of the situation and the circumstances of the letter, a smile touched Remy's lips. He'd forgotten the million and one times Aden had sworn Remy was out of his reach—like touching a star, Aden had claimed. Without that constant praise, Remy might not have won the title. Aden had given him confidence. Made him stand up taller.

There are a thousand things I should write in this letter, starting with how I failed you and ending with begging you not to hate me forever. But everything in my head is so goddamn ugly right now. Every time I try to start that letter, I end up tossing it. Instead, I want to talk about your eyes.

Remy's smile grew as he read.

Here, in Dublin, there's this lake, and when the light hits it just right, it's the same colour as your eyes. The first time we met, I felt ten years younger because your eyes reminded me of home. Then you opened your mouth, and I felt fifteen years too old to want you as badly as I did.

Remy swallowed hard, hoping he didn't cry. He couldn't stop the feelings racing through him.

You didn't notice me right away. Obviously, you saw me as your trainer, but you didn't look at me the way I always looked at you until six months after you signed up for my program. I'm not sure why you noticed me that night. It's almost funny that you did. I'd told myself earlier that same day I needed to let go of the fantasy of having you. You were becoming an obsession to me. I worried if you started seeing someone, I'd snap his neck.

A chuckle slipped from Remy without his permission. He could see Aden saying such a thing.

I'm twelve years older than you. Every day, I was hyper-aware of that age gap, until the day you kissed me.

Remy lifted his gaze from the letter and met Aden's stare. "You kissed me first," he said before going back to reading. At the next line, a low laugh escaped him.

I know you'll argue I kissed you first, but it was you. You were sitting on my desk and I went to reach past you for something—I can't even remember what now—

*and I think you thought I was coming in for a kiss. I
wasn't. You kissed me.*

"Are you fucking kidding me? All this time, I
thought you made the first move, and it was me?"

Aden's eyes shone bright with laughter. "Sorry. It
was you. If it makes you feel any better, I'm definitely
the one who swiped everything from the desk, intent
on getting inside you."

Remy sniffed, trying to decide if he was mollified. "I
suppose." He went back to reading.

*With one brush of lips on lips, you blew me away.
All the fantasies I'd had about you were nothing compared to the real thing. I wanted to crawl under your
skin and live there. Before that kiss, I honestly thought
I'd been in love a time or two in my life. Once our lips
met, I knew the truth. You were the first real love I'd ever
experienced. It didn't matter that you hadn't noticed me
before that night or if you'd ever return my feelings. You
made me groan in exasperation and laugh aloud at your
ridiculous antics. When you were around, I smiled and
dreamed. I hoped.*

Remy blinked, trying to make the page come back into focus after his eyes filled with tears. His heart ached like it would never be happy again because he remembered those days too clearly. He wanted them back.

Honestly, I don't imagine I'll ever send this letter. A huge part of me thinks I'll get better and, when I do, I'll hunt you down and dog your heels until I've made you see my life is meaningless without you. The thing is, I noticed your eyes first. I can still close my eyes and picture the way you looked at me when you told me you loved me. Damn, Remy, I don't know if I can survive replacing that image with one of how you'll look at me when you tell me you hate me.

It was getting harder not to cry. When Aden had ripped his heart out, Remy had been furious. He'd been angrier and more hurt than he'd ever been in his life, but nothing compared to how he'd felt when Aden tried killing himself. Every day, he'd fought the urge to hop the first flight and sit outside the rehabilitation center.

They wouldn't have let Remy see him, but goddamn. He wanted to be there and wished things were different.

I can't think about that right now. One day at a time, right? Instead, I think I'll go to bed and remember that kiss. Damned if you didn't kiss me like you'd been fantasizing about me too. Jesus. I miss you.

Remy flipped through the rest of the pages. Each one had a theme. The next was his smile. There was one about his hands. He almost stopped to read that one because it was a lot naughtier than the rest. Instead, Remy set the letters aside and focused on Aden. The man's expression bordered on crazed. It was obvious he was braced for any reaction from Remy.

"Do you trust me?"

Aden didn't hesitate. "Yes."

"Strip." This was the only way Remy knew how to fix the fear in Aden's eyes.

Without missing a beat, Aden pushed his chair away from the table and peeled his clothes off item by item until he stood nude.

"Sit down."

Aden sat.

"Don't move."

Remy swore Aden held his breath at the order. He tried not to think about what he was doing. In fact, Remy tried to keep his mind completely blank. That letter—fuck. It didn't answer any of the questions he wanted to ask, but fuck. In the bedroom, he quickly found what he was looking for and headed back to the table. Aden still sat where Remy left him. If Remy wasn't mistaken, the man hadn't moved a muscle. Remy bit his lip to keep from laughing.

"Do you remember our last Valentine's Day together?"

Aden's chest expanded. Oh yeah, he remembered. "Aye."

"Do you still trust me that much?"

"Aye. I'd trust you with everything."

"Good," Remy said. Even to his ears, he sounded breathless. He urged Aden's wrists to the arms of the chair and wound a belt around each one, holding the man in place. Remy prayed he still had the same patience he'd shown back then. This torture wasn't Aden's alone. If anything, it was worse on Remy. Aden's dick was already hard and standing at attention. "You know how this works," Remy reminded him. "Scoot all the way to the edge of the chair."

Aden slumped down in his seat until he ass nearly hung from the chair. Remy pushed the table away from them. Once he made room for another chair, he pulled up a seat and sat down across from Aden. Remy opened the bottle of lube he'd brought with him from the bedroom. After dumping a huge amount into his palm, Remy wrapped his fingers around Aden's cock, smearing oily liquid all over the man's skin. With Aden's dick coated in the shiny liquid, Remy dipped lower, ensuring the man's balls and asshole got the same treatment. One handful of lube wasn't enough for Remy. He wanted Aden washing for ten minutes to get all this stuff off later.

Aden's hips left the chair when Remy added a second hand to the mix. He pumped the man's cock with one hand while massaging Aden's balls with the other. Aden never broke eye contact. Remy's dick beat at the zipper on his pants. He ignored the discomfort. The unabashed way Aden owned his pleasure was mesmerizing. His ass left the seat, chasing after Remy's touch. Aden's mouth opened in a silent scream. His muscles strained. He fucked Remy's fist, openly taking everything he wanted. Remy jacked and twisted with one hand. With the other, he massaged Aden's asshole. The man's moans filled the room. Remy slipped one finger inside Aden's ass.

"Shit. Oh my God," Aden cried. His every hard line stood out under the strain. Remy purposely slowed his pace, pulling Aden away from the edge. Even as he kept Aden from orgasming, Remy worked another finger inside Aden's ass.

"You're so fucking sexy, darling," Remy praised. The effort Aden made to hold eye contact showed how strong Aden's will was. "I honestly think I could ignore my body's needs forever to see to yours. That's how much I love watching you on the edge."

"When I get inside you, I'm going to make you beg," Aden promised. His voice had turned guttural.

"I don't doubt it."

"You'll scream my name."

126

Remy's lips twisted into a smirk. "I always do."

Aden's eyes fell closed for a moment. His nostrils flared. When his eyes reopened, Remy's stomach tied into knots. Remy pumped Aden's cock at a snail's pace while fucking the man with his fingers.

"Tell me what you want from me." Remy's demand came out in a harsh whisper. Even he wasn't sure if he meant the question sexually. Since the second Aden arrived, Remy had craved knowing why Aden was there. He didn't know how much more of this his heart could stand.

"Everything."

Remy pulled away, leaving Aden hanging. "That's not a good enough answer."

Aden's nostrils flared again. "I want your gorgeous tight ass riding my dick until we're both raw from the punishment. I need to hold your stare as I fill your hole with my hot cum."

Remy stood. Aden's chin lifted, as if the man was incapable of looking away from Remy. Remy's hands went to the button on his shorts. Aden's dick twitched. He'd planned to go slow, dragging out Aden's torment. Aden's expression made it impossible. The flush on his cheeks. His swollen lips from chewing on them. It was too much temptation. Remy's clothes fell away. He didn't want to be in control any longer. Remy needed Aden's rough edges. He craved being fucked hard, losing himself in Aden's passion.

Before he could change his mind, Remy set Aden free. The instant Aden could move, he took Remy to the floor. Remy didn't try to slow things down. He reveled in Aden's rough treatment, his biting kisses. Aden's fingers dug into Remy's thigh as he shoved Remy's knee up. His tongue filled Remy's mouth, cutting off Remy's cries as his dick filled Remy's ass. The moment he was fully seated, Aden's mouth moved to Remy's ear. His ragged breaths brought chill bumps to Remy's skin.

"I love you, Remy. Goddamn, my heart. I love you."

Remy heard the words all the way to his soul. He believed Aden meant them, but Remy couldn't say it back. It wasn't that he didn't feel the same about Aden. The uncertainty of their future had Remy trying to protect his heart in any way he could. Instead, he captured Aden's mouth. Aden hit all the right places. Incapable of standing another second, Remy palmed his dick and stroked. Between Aden's cock filling his ass and the sensation of jacking himself off, Remy knew he wouldn't last long. He was already on edge from playing with Aden. Aden shifted, deepening his strokes. Remy's orgasm hit. His deep moan vibrated through their kiss. Aden tore his mouth away. His face was near to being animalistic. Waves of ecstasy rolled through Remy. His asshole contracted around Aden's dick.

"That's it, my heart. Milk me dry. You're so feckin' hot and tight. I want to stay here all night."

Remy swore his eyes glazed over at Aden's words. Lust choked him. Another wave of pleasure overtook him. The cords in Aden's neck stood out as the man tossed his head back, straining toward release. Remy couldn't look away. When Aden's orgasm finally hit, Remy swore he heard angels sing.

Cum smeared across their stomachs as Aden lowered his weight on Remy. Remy held on, uncaring if he could breathe. The sound of Aden placing light kisses on the shell of Remy's ear had Remy's lips turning up into a smile.

"Damn, my heart," Aden whispered against his ear. "I love you." Remy's eyes fell closed and his grip tightened. Another soft kiss landed across his ear. "It's okay," Aden whispered. "I love you enough for the both of us." Hot tears pressed at the backs of Remy's eyes. In that moment, everything Remy had lost was clearer than ever before.

Chapter 6

This time, there were two—Paper Pete and Chef Charlie. Paper Pete was still enjoying his banana. Chef Charlie had the white hat and all. Aden didn't rush through his breakfast as he'd done the day before. Instead, he stared at the two pictures of Remy—sitting side by side—and savored the moment. It was getting close to time for him to go home. There was every probability Remy wouldn't see him again after this trip. Maybe they were healing the past and not working toward any sort of future. Aden didn't intend to let a single chance at making a new memory pass him by. Sometimes, having a little of something wonderful was better than nothing at all. For so long, his last memory of Remy had been Remy's hatred. If he never saw Remy again after this week, at least he could live with himself again.

He chose to drive to No Rival again. This time, he had a plan. He'd enjoyed having dinner waiting on Remy. Perhaps he could do even more for the man tonight. The underground parking lot was packed, making it hard for Aden to find a parking spot, and to his surprise, while searching, he spotted Remy's car in the lot. Even after fighting for a place to park, Aden was still surprised by the massive number of people filling the club to capacity. Photographers milled around, taking pictures of everyone. Dozens of kids, wearing matching T-shirts, waited patiently for autographs and photo-ops. Equipment had been shoved back out of the way, making room for backdrops. For several minutes, Aden stared at the crowd, unsure of what to do. Finally, he spotted Drew headed in his direction.

"Aden, you made it."

Aden tried working up a smile. "Aye. What did I make it to?"

Drew's rumble of laughter brought a genuine smile to Aden's lips. "Did Remy not tell you? I'm always hosting some sort of charity event. This one is for kids who've lost their parents to violent crime. They come in and get their pictures made with the guys. The men sign autographs for them. Of course, the media comes out and draws attention to a worthy cause. Fun is had all around. Now that you're here, I'm assuming you won't be opposed to signing some autographs and joining in to help."

"Anything for a good cause," Aden said, because what other choice did he have? Plus, he liked helping to raise awareness where he could.

Drew slapped him across the back. If they hadn't

been so well matched in size, the man might've knocked Aden off his feet in his enthusiasm. "If you have a minute, I'd like to run something else by you, if I could?"

Aden nodded. "No problem."

After moving closer, Drew's expression turned serious. His gray eyes locked on Aden and didn't move. "I know you have your own place down south, but it's obvious there's something between Remy and you." He trailed off, as if hoping Aden would fill him in on the details. When Aden didn't volunteer any information, Drew cleared his throat. "Anyhow, I'm hoping whatever is going on with you two, it'll give you some incentive to stay. See, I'm retiring soon."

"No."

Drew shook his head. "You didn't let me finish."

"Apologies. It was a knee-jerk reaction. Go on," Aden said, trying to sound like an adult.

Instead of immediately picking up where he left off, Drew spent a moment eyeing Aden, as if ensuring he wouldn't interrupt again. "You could make a lot of money working for me."

"No."

A bright smile lit Drew's face. "For a moment there, I really thought you'd let me finish."

Aden nodded. "I'm trying. My mouth has other plans." He motioned for Drew to continue. "Just ignore me and keep going."

"I'd really like to sit down with you before you head back home and have a serious discussion about this. If you don't like Vegas, you wouldn't need to stay here. I'm talking about a partnership. There're five men here who are awesome and ready to take turns at training in my stead, but let's face it—they're not me or you. So, I was thinking, maybe I could send some men down your way for a boot-camp-type deal, where you fill in the blanks in their training."

As Aden listened to Drew's plan, each breath he took came harder than the last. His chest rose and fell—expanding a bit wider with each inhalation. He didn't want to panic, but the walls were closing in. There was no way Drew couldn't see he was freaking the fuck out, but Aden didn't believe the man would quit pushing until he was honest. The man obviously had a stubborn streak a mile wide.

"There's a reason I'm not the trainer to the stars any longer."

"I know," Drew said, stopping Aden before he was forced to say the words. "If you hang around long enough, you'll realize I know everything about everyone who steps through my door. Just think about it, okay? You don't have to let me know today." Drew stepped away. "Hang out. Sign some autographs. Get to know the guys on a more personal level and come out to the desert with us tonight for the burning of the horses. You'll find we're more of a family than a business—a family you might find it harder to walk away from than you think."

Aden nodded. His earlier panic subsided, turning into morbid curiosity. Apparently, they would be burning horses. "I'll think about it," Aden promised before Drew walked away. Aden wasn't one-hundred-percent sure that was true. When he'd walked away from training anyone other than Gunnar, Aden hadn't looked back nor did he care to do so now. The thing was—he loved Remy. He wasn't sure he wouldn't go back to hell to be with him.

*

It didn't occur to Remy until after he arrived at No Rival that he hadn't let Aden know the club would be closed to people working out today. He should've left him a note, but he'd been too busy making the man's breakfast and positioning all his photos just right. Several times he'd thought to text Aden, but he didn't want to wake him. After all, Remy had kept the man up all

135

night. An evil smile tugged at Remy's lips at the thought. He regretted nothing.

"Remy Bergeau."

Remy turned at the sound his name. Daniel headed his way. "Daniel Long," Remy said, faking a bright tone.

"Can I get your autograph?"

A snort escaped Remy. "I feel like we have this conversation at least twice a month. Shouldn't you have it already?"

Daniel shrugged. "I plan to keep asking until you add your phone number at the bottom." Surprise rendered Remy mute, which was just as well, since Daniel wasn't finished. "*The Sports Report* pays for my travel, and I had no intention of missing Drew Alexander or one of his many grand charity events. They're always a blast. Plus, you're here, and that's always fun too." The heat in Daniel's light-brown gaze couldn't be missed as it swept down Remy's body.

Remy had nothing.

Daniel's smile turned devilish. "So you really never guessed I have a thing for you? That's adorable. I guess I'll hang out just the same. Maybe once you let that bit of knowledge sink in, you'll choose to have dinner with me after the bonfire tonight."

Seriously, Remy had nothing.

"By the way," Daniel said, as if he hadn't dropped a major bombshell on Remy. "Did Aden Dawley ever get in touch with you? We had an interview a few days back, and he asked where you were training now. I got the impression he intended to come see you. Is he looking to start training you again now that Gunnar and Boston have found their way down south?"

"I'm confused," Remy said because it was true. "Are you hitting on me, digging for a scoop, or... what?" He knew he sounded every bit at a loss as he was, but it couldn't be helped.

"Well, like I said, *The Sports Report* pays for all my travel. If I want to keep enjoying that little benefit, I have to make it worth their while. But, yeah, I'm also totally hitting on you. I'd have to be a complete idiot not to at least try, right?"

It wasn't that Daniel was a bad-looking guy. In fact, Daniel was always styled to perfection and obviously kept in shape. He might even give Remy a run for his money in a beauty pageant, but that wasn't what Remy wanted in a man.

"There you are."

Remy startled as Aden appeared over Daniel's shoulder. He'd been transfixed while trying to decide how to deal with the reporter suddenly declaring himself. Aden had gotten the drop on him. Now there was two of them, and Remy still didn't know how to react.

Daniel didn't as much as flinch. His professional and practiced smile popped into place as he turned to greet the new arrival. "Aden. I was just asking Remy if you'd contacted him yet."

"Aye," Aden said, sounding sexy as sin. "I appreciate your help locating him." Aden's gaze flickered in Remy's direction and stayed. Remy's mouth went dry. He knew, before Aden reached past Daniel and snagged his hand, what would happen next. Aden hauled him closer. Remy went without protest. Things were so different between them now. They were the way they should've been years ago. No secrets. No hiding. Remy didn't hesitate meeting Aden halfway. When Aden lowered his head, Remy automatically went up onto his toes. Their lips met. Remy forgot where they were or who was watching. It was a quick kiss, but he couldn't stop smiling when Aden pulled away. "I enjoyed my breakfast with Paper Pete this morning. Oh, and why the bloody hell are we burning horses in the desert tonight?"

Remy threw his head back and roared with laughter. The way Aden asked the question—like he'd been scared to ask anyone else why they were performing some terrible voodoo ritual—had Remy swiping his eyes.

"It's an old Hong Kong tradition," Daniel said, reminding Remy of his presence. "Normally, it takes place on New Year's Day, but it's only in fun."

Aden tucked Remy against his side and focused on Daniel. "I can't imagine it's fun for the horses."

Daniel's smile was infectious. He didn't seem the least bit put-off by the fact that Aden and Remy were obviously together. "They're made of paper, so they don't put up much of a fuss. It's actually a pretty ingenious way to raise quite a bit of money. A huge crowd gathers in the desert for a massive bonfire. The horses are sold at two hundred dollars apiece. You decorate your horse with your wishes and throw it on the fire. The smoke carries your wish up to the gods. All the proceeds go to the local children's hospital."

Aden nodded, looking thoughtful. "That's much better than what I pictured. What brings you to town?"

"Remy," Daniel said, shocking the hell out of Remy. "I can't get my fill of writing his story."

Remy's gaze moved between the two men, expecting anything. He'd never been more confused. To his surprise, Aden smiled. "I told Remy you had a thing for him."

The desire to cover his heated cheeks rose in Remy. Neither man paid him any mind.

Daniel winked. "Seems we both have impeccable taste."

"Aden."

At the sound of Drew calling his name, Aden waved in the man's direction. His lips touched Remy's temple. "Sorry, my heart. It's time to earn my keep."

Remy nodded. "Talk to you later."

Aden dipped his chin in Daniel's direction. "Daniel."

"Aden," Daniel said with laughter lacing the word as Aden walked away. The second Aden was out of earshot, Daniel focused on Remy. "Hey, he didn't call me a little bastard this time. Progress."

A snort of laughter escaped Remy before he could call it back. "Sorry," he said quickly before Daniel could run away. "I should've told you we're together before you asked me to dinner."

Daniel waved off the apology. "I'm too fascinated to be upset. There's never been a name of any kind linked to Aden's. I thought he was straight. Seriously. He's so rough and tumble." Daniel's eyes flashed with humor. "Come to think of it, I may hate you a little at the moment. For real, I thought he was a monk or had traded his sex life soul for the ability to turn every fighter he trained into a star." A gasp left Daniel as if an extraordinary thought occurred to him. "I want all the details."

The need to know in Daniel's voice had Remy swiping his eyes and dying with laughter. "No fucking way am I giving you any specifics so you can print them and make a buck."

"I would never," Daniel said, sounding offended. "Okay, I would, but not this time. I need to know there's hope for love in this world. Did you see each other again and hit things off?" Daniel waved his arms wildly. "Oh my god, are you reunited lovers? Is he the one?"

141

"Yes."

Daniel laughed. "Yes to which one?"

An evil-sounding chuckle escaped Remy. For a moment, he wondered if he was mean enough to not answer. In the end, he couldn't deny the situation to anyone. "Yes. He's the one."

*

Aden spent the day switching between shaking hands, taking pictures, and watching Remy with Daniel. The two spent the entire day together. Several times, jealousy tried sneaking its way in, but Remy was smiling. The man had smiled the whole time. Soon Aden would head home. He couldn't stay here. Aden could already feel the pressure of this lifestyle choking him. At least a dozen times, he'd caught himself on the verge of hyperventilation. Aden wouldn't make it six months in this town before he'd be back to his old ways. That wasn't an option. He'd rather see Remy with someone else than trap the man with an addict again.

Daniel wasn't horrible. He had a good job. Most likely, he could work from anywhere. If he was dating Remy, he'd make Remy look good in the media. They'd be the perfect couple. Aden rubbed a spot in the center of his chest where an unexpected ache hit. He could survive knowing Remy was with someone else as long as Remy was happy. Really. He could. Aden tore his gaze away from the pair. He didn't need to convince himself of everything today. After all, Aden had the rest of his life—alone—to come to terms with some things.

"Let's drop your rental at the hotel and take my car to the bonfire."

Aden glanced over in surprise when Remy appeared at his side. He'd been watching the man so intently all day, he couldn't believe Remy had gotten the drop on him. "Sounds good. Is it time to leave already?"

Remy's arms slipped around Aden's waist as he tucked himself beneath Aden's arm. "Yeah. If we want to make it out there on time and drop off your car, we'll have to head out."

Aden didn't need to be told twice. It didn't occur to him to look for Daniel until after they headed for the door. He didn't see the man anywhere. "What about the little bastard reporter?"

A low chuckle rumbled from Remy's chest. Aden loved that sound. "He's going with Drew and Drew's wife, Aubree. He likes keeping Aubree entertained while Drew does the hosting thing. No doubt his willingness to stick with Aubree is the reason he keeps getting invited back."

"How very jaded you sounded right then," Aden said with a laugh.

"If the designer shoe fits," Remy muttered under his breath. Aden caught every word. Before Aden could comment, Remy continued. "It's nothing against Daniel. We all have our strengths. His is people. Everyone likes him and tells him things. They know he'll print every word but keep talking anyway. It's a gift. Anyhow," Remy said, obviously set on changing the subject as they hit the parking lot. "Since you weren't there when they were selling the paper horses for the event, I bought two. They're pretty big. I thought while I decorate one side of one, you could decorate one side of the other, and then we can switch. One can be our wishes for other people, and one can be our wishes for ourselves. What do you think?"

Aden thought Remy looked excited by the idea, and that was enough for him. "I think those are some expensive horses. You should let me pay you back."

Remy waved off his words. "Bringing up money with me is ridiculous. Get going. I'll meet you at the hotel."

Aden took a step back. It was stupid. They were headed to the same place and would be together again in five minutes, but he didn't want to walk away. "Maybe I should leave my car here and get it tomorrow. You know, so we're not late." Remy's gorgeous smile had Aden closing the gap between them again. Without thought, he covered Remy's mouth with his. Their tongues met. The tension eased from Aden's shoulders.

"You're right," Remy said against his lips. "Get in the car."

He didn't wait for Remy to change his mind. Aden circled the car and climbed into the passenger seat the moment Remy unlocked the doors. Once they were on the road, Remy reached over and linked his fingers through Aden's before bringing Aden's hand to his mouth. Remy kept his gaze locked on the road. His lips remained pressed to Aden's hand. Silence engulfed them. It seemed fitting somehow they should enjoy this moment of peace—like it was owed to them.

Since they were the first to leave, they were also the first to arrive. Only the crew who'd been hired to set up the event was there. Neither of them moved from the car. With the vehicle running, saving them from the heat outside, and the radio playing softly, they sat side by side. They toyed with each other's fingers, weaving a spell.

"I know I fucked things up," Aden said, incapable of holding his tongue a second longer. "But you were the one for me."

Remy looked over and their gazes met. The man's mouth lifted in one corner in a sad smile. "If we never see each other again after my match, I need you to know, you've been the one for me too."

The claim hit Aden's soul. He loved this man, and Aden couldn't live with knowing he'd said the words to Gunnar and not Remy. So he let the words fall between them. "I won't be searching for another. It's not that I'm punishing myself or any such nonsense. I just don't want anyone else."

Remy nodded but didn't respond. More cars arrived, breaking the spell.

"I guess we should get out," Aden suggested.

Once again, Remy nodded. Neither of them moved. "Thank you," Remy said before Aden could be the first one to exit the car, as he'd thought to do.

"For what?"

"Loving me," Remy said, sounding confident in that belief. "Maybe we failed in the most spectacular way, but you also loved me in the most beautiful display." With a shake of his head and while still smiling, Remy climbed from the car. Aden did too because his body was on auto-pilot and following Remy's lead. His mind remained locked on Remy's words. He was right. Maybe they'd failed, but goddamn it, they'd been feckin' beautiful.

*

People didn't trickle into the burning of the horses. Most everyone left No Rival at the same time and poured into the desert at the same rate. Once people started showing up, things moved quickly. Being the first to arrive meant they got their horses first. Aden decorated one while Remy worked on the other. When they switched, Remy peeked. There was no stopping himself. The instant Aden handed over his horse, Remy flipped it over and checked out Aden's drawing.

His first reaction was to snort. Neither of them needed to quit their day job. It didn't matter if Aden's doodling made sense, because he'd added cliff notes. All of Remy's personalities stared back at him. Crossfit

Chad, Paper Pete, and Chef Charlie. Aden had written their names beneath each stick figure. Each one was smiling. Remy would know. Aden had drawn an arrow to each of their faces with the same note. "Notice the smile? I wish it was permanent."

Remy took a deep breath and swallowed past the lump in his throat. When he glanced up, he found Aden watching him. The man's expression matched the way Remy felt. No one else would ever want as much for them as they wanted for each other. Remy knew exactly what he'd wish for Aden.

First, he drew a house with a sun and waves. Next came two stick figures holding hands. He gave one of the stick figures glorious hair because that was important. Finally, he drew a big red heart on each figure's chest. He gave each heart stitches. Otherwise, they'd never mend. With his illustration complete, Remy looked Aden's way. He was finished too.

"Which one do you want to toss on the fire?"

"That one," Aden said, pointing at the horse Remy was holding and making Remy breathe a sigh of relief. He was dying to see what else Aden had drawn but didn't want to ask. The instant they swapped horses, Remy inspected Aden's second wish. It was exactly the same as the first.

Remy froze. "You were supposed to wish for something for yourself."

"I did," Aden argued, sounding unconcerned. "There's nothing I want more than to see you happy." He held Remy's drawing up, flashing it Remy's way. "Is this supposed to be us?"

Remy eyed the picture he'd just drawn. Two men. Both with broken hearts on the mend and one with perfect hair. It wasn't as if Remy could deny the likeness. "I should've given you awesome hair too, or clown feet."

"Are we in Key Largo?"

Remy eyed the house next to the waves. "Personally, I would've asked about the clown feet, but yeah, I suppose we are."

Aden didn't crack a smile. "Is this what you want?"

Remy shrugged. Their discussion was getting too real, and Aden didn't look happy. "It's what I want for you."

"But not for you, right?" Aden asked, sounding angry.

Before he could stop himself, Remy snatched the horse from Aden's hands and tossed both paper ponies on the fire. He didn't bother watching them burn. Without a word or looking Aden's way, he headed for the car. Remy's sudden shit mood wasn't Aden's fault. He'd been a fucked up mess for a while. Part of Remy wanted to scream "yes." Yes, he wanted that beautiful life on the beach with Aden. But he was scared shitless to give up everything he'd worked so hard to achieve for a man who might not stay clean or faithful. There were so many things he wanted to yell at the top of his lungs. If he ever started, he might not stop.

Aden overcame him at the car. Remy knew, in truth, Aden had probably waited until they were out of sight before pulling Remy back against his chest and engulfing Remy in his embrace.

"Come find me," Aden said, sounding sure and steady. "When you're ready, come home to me. I wasn't talking out my ass earlier. For the rest of my life, it'll be you. If you can ever forgive me, I'll be in the house on the beach, waiting."

He fucking meant it. Every word. Remy could hear it in Aden's voice. He didn't know if he should melt into Aden's touch or stomp the man's toes. How dare Aden give up the rest of his life to loving Remy? Remy's shoulders fell. Why couldn't Remy say the words that would bridge the gap between them?

"It's okay," Aden said quietly against Remy's neck. Aden's soothed his fears as if he could read Remy's mind. "Stop worrying over my feelings." He gently turned Remy in his arms until their gazes met. Aden inspected Remy's face and a small smile touched Aden's lips. His fingertips skimmed Remy's cheek. "Damn," Aden breathed. "I owe you so much. You are the most amazing person. Why didn't I tell you that every single day?"

A smile that surprised even him stretched Remy's lips. "You did. Every single day. You told me I was beautiful and brightened the world. Thousands of times you said I was better than everyone and made a point of grabbing my butt every day. I always knew I was wanted."

Aden's hands slid down Remy's back. His expression turned wicked as he grabbed two handfuls of Remy's ass. "So... the windows of your car are tinted pretty dark."

"I like my privacy," Remy said. His desire grew.

"My guess is—I could get inside you and no one would see."

"Probably," Remy said, but they'd done a lot of hiding and sneaking around during their time together. They didn't need to do that now. "But if we leave right now, we could be home in less than fifteen minutes. Then I'd be free to do some freaky shit to you."

"Isn't it my turn to be the deviant? It's been a long time since I did that thing with my tongue. You know how I—"

Remy pulled out of Aden's hold. "Get in the car, darling. You're in for a long night." He meant it too. Remy's dick was already begging for Aden's attention and fifteen minutes sounded like a long time. He needed to get this man alone before he climbed Aden like a tree and fucked him like a monkey for all the world to see. God knew, with Daniel there, it would likely end up as front-page news.

Chapter 7

A warm weight shifted at Aden's back. The corners of his mouth tugged, attempting to pull his lips into a smile before his eyes opened. Hoping he wouldn't wake Remy, Aden rolled over. The first sight of Remy, sleeping peacefully at Aden's side, caused the air to race from his lungs. Every time he thought he fully grasped all he'd lost, another moment came, reminding him there was more.

After moving closer, Aden draped his arm over Remy. As he'd done countless times in the past, Remy automatically snuggled into Aden's hold. Aden's throat tightened. This was his final day. His last morning. Remy would do his pre-fight weigh-ins, countless interviews, and pace the floor. After Remy's fight tonight, Aden would fly home. Chances were good, he wouldn't even get to see Remy when the match ended. There'd be a ton of reporters expecting a press conference and the crowd would rush him off to some after party event. This was it for them. Aden held on for as long as he could. He knew the exact moment Remy woke. When the man didn't move away, Aden counted it as a victory. For a long time, they held each other in silence. In truth, there wasn't much left to say. Aden had given his best. Now Remy would see him again or he wouldn't.

"What time is weigh-in?'

"One," Remy said. His tone gave nothing away.

"What time are you headed over?"

He felt Remy shrug. "There's no sense in leaving before twelve thirty. If I get there early, it'll mean more interviews and signing shit. Sponsors will want pictures of me with their products. I'd rather not get started any earlier than necessary."

Aden glanced at the clock beside the bed. "So I have three hours to spoil you before you go."

"You don't have to do that."

He didn't. Aden knew that already, but not only did he want to, he could hear the smile in Remy's voice. Aden needed to keep the man happy like water was a requirement to live. After placing a long and noisy kiss to the side of Remy's neck, Aden climbed from the bed.

"Don't move from that spot," he ordered. Aden took two steps before a thought struck and he paused. "Unless you're making a quick trip to the bathroom. You're allowed that. Otherwise, you're to stay in bed."

"If you're forcing me," Remy said on a laugh. "I guess I'll suck it up and be lazy."

"Aye, you will," Aden said, using his bossiest tone. He didn't wait to see if Remy complied. It was his turn to make breakfast.

*

After enjoying an amazing breakfast together, Aden made Remy stay put at the kitchen table while he disappeared into the bedroom. Remy humored him. His gaze strayed to the chair where he'd teased Aden the night before last. The belts still dangled from the chair's arms. Housekeeping had come and gone since then. He wondered what they thought of the sight. A smile touched Remy's lips before slowly fading away. This was it for them. They could talk about trying to make things work between them, but they now lived on opposite sides of the country. Aden couldn't move here. Even if the man was willing, Remy couldn't let him. The last thing Aden needed was to slip back into the life they'd had before. Key Largo was a small town with minimal pressure. Just what Aden needed to stay well. Here, the success was everything. Remy couldn't go back to loving an addict.

The muscles in Remy's stomach clenched at the

thought. He never let himself think about what those days had been like. Most of the time, their relationship had been a normal one. Aden had been using for so long he'd become a high-functioning addict. That sounded like it wasn't as bad as a junkie who lived in the streets, always searching for the next high. It wasn't better. In fact, it was terrifying, because Aden could hide his problem. He could hold entire conversations with people without giving himself away. Get behind the wheel of a car. Train a man to fight. Pass out and die.

Remy had lived in constant fear of waking up next to a dead man. No one could understand the terror unless they'd been there. Loving an addict was emotional blackmail. He couldn't leave Aden because addiction is an illness. Remy never had the option to walk away. His heart equally didn't care Aden was sick. Love had trapped Remy like a giant spider web and he'd lain still—unsure of which way it would destroy him.

Aden reappeared. The man's T-shirt strained against his muscles. His workout shorts left nothing to the imagination, letting Remy know Aden hadn't bothered with underwear. It hit Remy—that giant web had ensnared him again at some point in the last few days.

His heart turned over in his chest. In what way would Aden destroy him this time? Remy already wasn't the same.

His chin lifted as Aden moved closer until he was staring up at Aden hovering over him. "Come on, my heart," Aden said, taking Remy's hands. "It's bath time."

Remy chewed his bottom lip as Aden pulled him to his feet. Emotion weighed so heavily on Remy's shoulders, his every step felt awkward. The large garden tub came into view. Water filled the porcelain almost to the brim. Bubbles and steam called Remy's name as Aden helped strip Remy's clothes away. As the water engulfed him, Remy mused over how it was the perfect temperature. It seemed wrong somehow for Aden to do everything so goddamn right. The knowledge hurt and Remy didn't even know why. Aden sat down beside the tub. He toyed with Remy's fingers. His silence was Remy's strength. That felt unfair, given the circumstances.

He didn't want this to end. Every second that passed was another inch in the gulf widening between them. Ugly thoughts crowded his brain. Remy couldn't understand why life had given him so much yet so little. He had more money than he could spend in two lifetimes thanks to holding the title for three years. Except for a few charities, he rarely spent a dime. All he did was go to No Rival and train to hold on to the title that brought him more money that he never spent. The ride was more of a merry-go-round than an adventure. In the back of his mind, Remy held tight to a secret. One he feared to ever speak. It felt wrong and ungrateful when so many other people struggled every day, but the truth was there—hiding. He hated his life. At the thought, Remy sucked in a deep breath, trying to lock down the pain. No one could ever know.

"Are you nervous about tonight?"

Remy tried pulling his head out of his ass at Aden's question. "Yeah."

"You've got nothing to worry about."

"I know," Remy said, because it was obvious Aden needed the reassurance.

"All you have to do is show up, and you'll have this fight won."

Remy could tell Aden was searching for a way to fix Remy's growing dark mood. Remy forced a smile for

Aden. He didn't want the man worrying. The problem was—Remy no longer knew if he cared to win. Aden's flight was leaving after Remy's fight and there was so much unsaid between them. Remy tried calming his nerves over the upcoming fight, but all he could think about was Aden going back to Key Largo. He'd be left behind again in this town where he couldn't fucking breathe. Remy didn't trust anyone anymore, and he didn't want to be anyone's friend. He no longer knew if this place sucked the life from him or if he hated everything everywhere.

Aden stood to leave. "I'll light some candles in the bedroom so you can relax there when you finish here."

He couldn't take any more of feeling like Aden tiptoed around him. "I dream about you," Remy said before Aden could get away. From the corner of his eye, Remy saw Aden freeze, but Remy couldn't look the man's way as he made his confession. "Do you remember how we used to buy each other a puzzle every year for Christmas? On Christmas day, we'd sit on the floor with you on one side of the coffee table and me on the other. We'd spend all day in silence, piecing together our puzzles while playing footsy under the table." Remy couldn't even smile at the memory because those days had turned into nightmares for him. "Since Cornerman was closed on Christmas, it was the one day in the year we were free to be together in peace without worrying someone would find out about us and you'd lose your job. At least once a week, I dream about those days together. Then I wake up, and for a few seconds, I live in blissful ignorance." Remy swallowed past the pain. He needed to have his say. "Since you left me, those beautiful memories have turned into something ugly. I thought we were working on making our own traditions. Now all I can do is wonder if what I thought was beautiful was really just boring the hell out of you."

Aden walked back to the edge of the tub and stood over Remy. His expression gave no clue to his thoughts. Remy didn't know why he couldn't stop rehashing things. He didn't understand why this lingering depression wouldn't let him go. Since Aden had shown up in Vegas, Remy wanted to set the past aside and try again. There was a weight sitting on his chest and crushing him that Remy couldn't seem to crawl out from underneath.

"I still have the last puzzle I bought you. It's all wrapped up and sitting on the shelf in my closet."

That hurt. It had been two weeks before Christmas

when Aden had tried to kill himself. Remy remembered the date well. His house had already been decorated. He'd torn down everything Christmas related, packed it up, and set it on the curb for the garbage men to pick up. He hadn't celebrated again since. Oh, he still went to see his mom and did the present exchange, but that was where the holidays ended for Remy.

Aden went down onto his knees beside the tub. "I think I need to say a lot of things to you I never wanted you to hear. The thing is, I don't want hurt you any-more, and I don't know which is worse—telling you eve-rything or pretending it didn't happen."

Remy held his silence because he couldn't make that decision. He was too rundown by life.

For a moment, Aden stared at some point over Remy's shoulder before meeting his gaze. He could tell by the hard set to Aden's jaw, he'd made his choice. "You were the reason I got up every morning. That is, when I actually slept. God knows, for a long time, I had nothing else to look forward to. Sometimes, I would go days when I didn't eat or sleep. Nobody knew. There was no peace or quiet in my life. The phone always rang. People wanted me to train them. Sponsors wanted me to train fighters they needed to win. The gym wanted me to make a star out of every single client no matter how unreasonable that request might be. Oh my God, Remy. I couldn't feckin' breathe."

He couldn't look away from Aden's expression. Remy understood what Aden meant. He hadn't taken a proper breath since winning the title three years ago.

Aden shook his head. "The only happiness I ever had was when I was with you. Even then, I wanted to do everything within my power to help you be a winner, because I needed you to have the world. Only then would it make sense for you to be with me. Otherwise, why the feck would you want to be with me. I was a bloody mess." Aden took a deep breath. His chest expanded with the motion, and Remy almost begged him not to say anything else. He knew he wouldn't like what Aden had to say—felt it in his bones. "When I woke up in that bed next to Boston, it was like the last good thing inside me shriveled and died." Aden crossed his arms over his stomach as if trying to protect himself from the memories. "I still wish I'd died," Aden whispered, bringing a rush of hot tears to Remy's eyes because of the pure honesty in Aden's confession. The man honest-to-God meant every word.

His lungs burned, making Remy realize he held his

breath.

"This life I have," Aden said, still whispering as if he couldn't say the words any louder or he might break. "It isn't worth a damned thing." Aden gripped the edge of the tub on either side of Remy and leaned in until only an inch separated them as if impressing his words upon Remy. "You have been the only good part of me. I was never bored. You were never lacking. I am the failure here and I am so goddamn sorry."

Because he couldn't stand it any longer, Remy snagged two handfuls of Aden's shirt and tugged, pulling the man forward. Their lips met. The world righted itself and Remy could breathe again. Aden climbed into the tub—shorts and all. Water splashed over the edge of the tub, pooling on the floor. Remy's laughter reverberated off the bathroom walls.

"Oh my God, crazy. What are you doing?"

While straddling Remy's hips, Aden sat back on his heels and reached over his head. He peeled his wet shirt up and over his head before tossing it aside. "Joining you," Aden answered before covering Remy's mouth once more with his. Remy savored the man's deep and seeking kiss before losing patience. He wanted to drape himself over Aden's body like a blanket and hang on forever. Remy pushed and shoved until he had Aden sitting opposite of him. After going up on his knees, he peeled the man's shorts down his hips.

"I hope your phone wasn't in your pocket."

Aden shook his head while watching Remy with a heated gaze. "I don't need my phone when you're around."

"Good," Remy said as he worked the shorts down Aden's hips. It wasn't easy, but Remy didn't stop until he had Aden nude. With the man's soaked clothes ruining the floor, Remy straddled Aden's hips and melted against him. He pressed his forehead to Aden's and stared into the man's gorgeous green eyes. Up close, he could make out the flecks of gold around the edges. Remy breathed deep. By tonight, Aden would be gone. He wanted to remember every detail. Because he couldn't resist, Remy captured Aden's mouth once more. He kept their kiss short. This wasn't about sex for him and they were both getting turned on.

"You're supposed to be relaxing," Aden fussed as Remy wiggled closer, finding a comfortable spot.

"I am." With his body pressed as close as he could get, Remy sank into Aden and buried his face against the man's neck. With steam rising around them and every inch touching, it was a perfect moment. Remy never wanted it to end.

"What do you want to do in our last two hours together?"

"This," Remy said, sounding tired even to his ears. "Just this."

The water turned colder as the minutes passed. He tried keeping his mind blank. It didn't work. Instead, Remy ran through every conversation they'd had since Aden came into town. He didn't want to have any regrets. If there was something he'd left unsaid, he needed to say it now before the water got cold and they were over. There was only one thing that came to mind that he knew he couldn't live without Aden knowing. "God help me. I still love you."

*

I still love you. Those words hadn't stopped running through Aden's head since they'd left Remy's mouth. From that moment on, the rest of the day became a haze for Aden. He'd thought he'd known what he'd be losing by going back home after Remy's fight. Turned out, Aden hadn't known shit. Drew's offer to stay was taking root in the back of Aden's mind, warring it out with what Aden knew was the right thing to do. He couldn't stay here. As much as he'd like to believe that loving Remy made him too strong to fall into old habits, he couldn't take that risk. Somehow, Remy's love had survived the last round. It wouldn't survive a second betrayal.

As Aden had predicted, the second Remy's weigh-in had been complete, he'd been swept away by a flood of reporters. The last Aden had seen of Remy, he'd been talking quietly with Daniel. At the sight, Aden had bitten back a snort. Remy had called it. It didn't matter if people knew Daniel would print every word they said, he still got all the goods.

Now, sitting surrounded by people he didn't know, Aden wondered why they'd chosen not to say goodbye. Any minute, Remy would finish final inspection with the judges and dip into the ring. It would be the last time Aden would set eyes on the man. *I still love you.* Damn. Life was unfair. It seemed wrong for such a beautiful love to be so destructive.

Remy ducked between the ropes and the crowd lost

their minds. Aden's chest swelled with pride. That was his baby, getting everything he deserved in life. Rules were read. Aden couldn't look away from Remy's expression. He looked eerily calm—not like he'd gone into fight mode, but like he wasn't even there. The muscles in Aden's stomach clenched. The bell rang, signaling the first round and Remy came out, landing the first blow. Aden's shoulders relaxed. He was seeing things that weren't there, projecting his nervousness on Remy. Remy was the clear winner. His every move was perfect.

Each round was timed at three minutes. By the eighth, Aden was ready to chew through the ropes. Remy bled under one eye but was leading in points and looked ten times in better shape than his opponent. That man was bleeding in at least four spots and looked ready to collapse at any moment. When round ten began, Aden's only consolation was that it was almost over. He wondered if he'd be the one who went down from the exhaustion of it all. One minute in, Remy's opponent drew back to strike. It was a slow movement—one obviously hindered by the man's weariness. Remy saw the move coming too. Aden had trained the man too long to misread his movements. He'd repositioned his hands, prepared to block. His feet shifted slightly. At the last second, Remy dropped his hands and took the hit. He went down. Aden's breath left his lungs. It wasn't possible. He'd seen it with his own eyes. But still, it wasn't possible. He listened to the count. Remy didn't budge. The count ended along with the match. Still, Aden couldn't look away from Remy. The man had thrown his match. It hadn't been an accident. The dude hadn't beaten Remy or thrown a lucky punch. Aden had watched Remy drop those hands at just the right moment. He'd purposely taken a dive. He'd lost the title.

Aden tried everything to make his way to the back and get to Remy. By the time he found someone he could charm with his credentials, it was only to be informed Remy had already left the building. Security had sneaked the man out the back as soon as the bout ended. Aden called. He texted. Tried going by the hotel. Remy was nowhere to be found. His flight was leaving. They were over. Remy's career was in the toilet and Aden didn't know how to feel. Mostly, he felt useless. This was the second huge milestone in Remy's life that Aden hadn't been allowed to be a part of. The night Remy had won the title, Cornerman gym had kept him away. Now, Remy had learned to live without him and obviously didn't need him. In the end, it didn't matter

168

how much Aden wanted to be a part of Remy's life. The man had disappeared, leaving Aden no other choice but to go home.

Chapter 8

Remy wiped his palms on his jeans before knocking. Damn, he'd never thought this day would come. Then again, his life hadn't been normal as of late. When the door swung wide, Remy almost took a step back. The man standing in the doorway was easily one of the most gorgeous men Remy had ever seen. His nervousness level shot through the roof.

"You must be Gunnar's husband. I'm sorry. I don't know your name."

The man's light green eyes sparkled with kindness. Remy felt sick. "Yes. I'm Liam."

Remy wiped his hands on his jeans again. "I'm Remy," Remy said, as if that explained anything to a complete stranger. Of course, there was also the possibility that Gunnar cursed his name every other day. "Is Gunnar around?"

Liam shook his head. His shaggy brown hair moved in time with the motion, looking soft and perfect. Still, Remy kind of wanted to style it differently. "Sorry. He went for a run a while ago, but he should be back any minute if you'd like to come inside and wait."

Remy took a step back at the offer. He tried smiling. Unfortunately, he feared it looked closer to a grimace. "No. Thank you. He wouldn't appreciate me being alone with you. I'll come back another time."

A deep line appeared between Liam's eyes. Even that was hot. "Okay. If you're sure? I'll tell him you stopped by."

Remy shook his head. "Please don't. Seriously, he'd be upset if he knew you spoke to me when he wasn't around."

"Oh, Remy, that's not true," Gunnar said behind him, startling Remy and sounding sad. Remy spun, catching sight of a sweat-soaked Gunnar. His first re-action was to turn away. He didn't want to be furious with Gunnar, but he was, so goddamn much. "Come in," Gunnar said. The heavy sigh in his voice, as if he knew Remy's thoughts, was what had Remy's feet moving. Liam stepped aside, letting Remy pass. Remy tried for a genuine smile and failed again. Even he wasn't sure why he was doing this to himself.

Liam motioned toward a dark leather couch. "Would you like something to drink?"

Remy shook his head, still trying to smile while

wondering if he looked like a crazy person. After choosing one end of the couch, Remy tried making himself as small as possible. "You have a beautiful home," Remy said to no one in particular. Honest to God, he didn't know what else to say.

"I saw you threw your fight the other night."

Remy's gaze shot to Gunnar's. His jaw was set in a hard line. So it was like that—no gloves. Remy could handle that. "You're a shitty friend."

Liam froze halfway between sitting and standing. He glanced between them and stood. "Well, I'm out." Neither Gunnar nor Remy argued as Liam slipped from the room, leaving them alone.

Remy held Gunnar's gaze, daring him to say something.

After a moment, Gunnar's shoulders fell. "I know."

The pain hit and Remy had to look away to keep from crumpling.

"When I came home unexpectedly, it was on purpose," Gunnar admitted, pulling Remy's gaze back his way. Gunnar's hands were balled into fists in his lap. His knuckles were white. Remy needed to hear what the man had to say. "You see, I knew there was something going on with Boston. I felt it in my gut, but I wasn't sure what it was. Was he cheating? Tired of me? Whatever, I just felt him pulling away, and I had to know. So I waited until I had an extra day between out of town bouts, and intentionally came home unannounced. Since I half expected to catch him at something and you were there, I didn't want to hear any explanations."

"We weren't sleeping together. I never would've done that to you."

Gunnar nodded. His hands relaxed. Remy watched as the white of his knuckles pinkened. "I know. Boston came by right after you showed up here in town. He told me everything. He said the two of you were arguing over the thing with Aden, and in the best—or worst, depending upon how you look at it—case of timing ever, I came in as he pushed you down on the bed to keep you from killing him."

Remy didn't know where to go with that. The Boston he knew was a self-serving bastard who cared about no one. He wasn't the type of person who made a special trip to his ex's house to clear another man's name. Gunnar kept talking, giving Remy time to think.

"I get why you didn't tell me right then that you were there to kill Boston for touching Aden, but why did you let me believe you were sleeping with him?"

Remy shrugged. "At the time, I hated everyone—Aden for cheating, Boston for his part, you for thinking me capable of such a thing and bringing Boston into our lives. Most of all—I hated myself for caring about any of you enough to let you break me."

"And now?"

The million-dollar question—the one he'd asked himself all the way there. "I love Aden." Remy's eyes filled with tears as he made the admission. His chest hurt. Loving Aden had almost killed him once already this lifetime, but Remy couldn't stop. "Help." Even to Remy's ears, he sounded desperate.

"Oh, lord, he's about to fall apart," Liam said, rushing across the room and proving he'd never really left. Remy didn't know the man but accepted his shoulder when Liam's arms surrounded him.

"I don't know what I'm doing anymore," Remy admitted against Liam's shoulder as if the man knew anything at all about him.

"Being a dumbass," Gunnar said, transforming

into the friend Remy had once loved. Remy peeked over Liam's shoulder and stared at Gunnar—waiting. He could handle being called a dumbass as long as someone told him what to do. When Gunnar saw he had Remy's attention, he continued, "Why do you think I refused to accept Boston's challenge for the title for so long? Because all the fame that goes along with it, that's no joke," Gunnar answered, obviously not expecting any input from Remy. "I never wanted it after seeing what it did to Aden and Boston. You're currently being held by the only reason I can handle the pressure of being a title holder."

"Awww," Remy cried against Liam's shoulder. "This makes me doubly glad to get to meet you today. Not like this, of course," Remy said, making Liam chuckle. He still didn't give the man up. Liam was a rather soft spot to fall, and he smelled nice too. Liam was peaceful. Nothing had been calm in Remy's life for years.

"You're not going to like hearing this," Gunnar said, ignoring Remy. "But you need to hear it. Back then, Aden was sick. He needed help that none of us could give him. Ending up in bed with Boston was the best and worst thing to happen to him."

Ouch.

"It saved his life, because he realized how much he'd rather be dead than keep hurting you. As fucked up as it sounds, you're a fucking idiot if you think you'll ever find anyone who'll love you more than that."

Double ouch.

"You came here for help. I'm giving it to you. That man loves you. No one will judge you for forgiving him and loving him back. I don't know about you, but I don't want to live in a world where, no matter how sorry you are, no one ever forgives anyone."

Remy forced himself to pull away from Liam. This time, he also managed a genuine smile for Liam before focusing on Gunnar. "I'm here, and I've pretty much thrown away my career, so I guess it's safe to say I've forgiven him. Unfortunately, I have no clue where to start with this."

Gunnar shrugged. "Wherever you're happiest, I suppose."

For the first time in a long time, Remy didn't feel like throwing up. He knew exactly where he was happiest.

*

The door to the gym was unlocked. That was just fucking fantastic. He went out of town for the first time in ages and had chosen to take a few days off when he got back home and look what happened. Everything went to shit. Either people had taken to breaking into his gym, or Gunnar was a big feckin' idiot who didn't know how to lock a door behind him. With his mood at total shit level, Aden stormed inside and locked the door at his back, because—unlike Gunnar—he knew how to turn a lock and it wasn't time to open. Every step he took toward the office felt a little harder until he was eating up the floor and stamping his feet.

He threw open his office door and froze. Every inch of bare wall was covered in sidewalk chalk. Giant hearts and suns joined clouds and trees. It was a crazy hot mess. Aden couldn't stop smiling. He automatically looked up, praying to see the words he needed. His grin widened at the hundreds of *"I love yous"* covering the entire ceiling. Remy was nowhere in sight. Aden searched the gym from top to bottom, finding it empty. He returned to his office and inspected each drawing. That was where he found the note, written by the light switch.

"Scuba Sam's having a dance party back at your place. P.S. You're invited."

Aden snorted. Only Remy would come up with a name as dumb as Scuba Sam. He headed for the door, uncaring of the day's schedule. Sometimes, saving your sanity was more important than paying the bills. He locked up and headed back for Surfside Way. He'd rather be at a dance party than anywhere else in the world.

A red Dodge Challenger with Nevada plates sat parked in Aden's driveway, explaining why Aden hadn't been able to locate Remy for the past five days. Even if the man had driven straight through without stopping—an impossible feat—it would've taken him three days. For Remy to be here now, when Aden had left for the gym not half an hour earlier, Remy had to have been lying in wait, watching for Aden's departure. Not to mention, the only way Remy could've gotten into his gym and his home was with Gunnar's help. People were plotting against him, and he loved it.

As Aden approached the door, the thump of loud music met him. Seemed Scuba Sam really was having a dance party. A smile pulled at Aden's lips at the thought. There was a newspaper article taped to the front door. It was an exclusive after-fight interview between Remy and Daniel. Aden skimmed its contents. He couldn't believe his eyes. Not once, but three times,

Remy contributed his success to falling in love with Aden. Aden paused to read.

The knowledge he [Aden Dawley] was there, in the background of my life and silently cheering me on, gave me the confidence to succeed. Now it's time for me to be there for him—for us.

Aden couldn't go another second without seeing Remy. The front door was unlocked and Aden found Remy in the living room. He choked back his laughter at the first sight of the man. Dressed in a wetsuit, flippers, and with goggles on his head, Remy switched between moonwalking and the Electric Slide.

"What's with the get-up?"

Remy turned at Aden's question, but didn't stop dancing. "I figure if I plan on beach bumming it from now on, then I'd better take up a hobby. Scuba diving sounds like fun."

The happiness was crushing him. Aden refused to wonder if Remy meant what Aden thought he meant. He needed a straight answer. "Does that mean you're staying for good?"

"Of course," Remy answered as if there was never a doubt. "I have conditions, but watch this." Remy peeled off the flippers and left them sitting side by side. After turning around, he backed up until his heels matched up with the backs of the flippers. Remy raised his arms and stuck out his ass before moving his hips in time with the music. "What am I?" he sang, before barking like a seal, and singing. "I'm a dancing seal." He barked again. "A dancing seal."

Inside his head, Aden laughed so hard he was holding the stitch in his side. Damned if Remy didn't look just like a skinny seal dancing to techno. On the outside, Aden held himself in check, because they had things to discuss. The longer he stared at Remy, the bigger his hunger grew. Without thought, he ate up the space between them. Aden kicked the flippers aside and snagged a dancing Remy around the waist. He hauled the man flush against him. Remy squirmed in his arms, refusing to stop dancing. Aden pulled the zipper down on the wetsuit, revealing Remy's bare skin underneath. He didn't stop until he could push the material down Remy's arms, trapping him inside its sleeves. With his prey held captive, Aden opened his mouth over the cords of Remy's neck. His dick twitched as Remy's ass gyrated against Aden's crotch. He was so in love with this crazy-ass man. There was no one else like Remy. That was why Aden needed to know everything.

"List your conditions so I can set them at your feet."

Remy stopped dancing and melted into Aden's touch, conforming to Aden's body. "I expect you to marry me."

"Done," Aden said, not sorry since Remy's first condition matched what would've been Aden's first demand. "What else?"

"If you break me, I get to cut off your dick."

Aden cringed out of habit but didn't back down. "I'll do it for you so you won't go to jail. Anything else?"

Remy somehow managed to snuggle closer. "No. I think I'm good with those two things. How about you? Would you like to add to negotiations before we close this deal?"

"I want the ridiculous you. Not the guy who lived in Nevada."

Remy barked again before agreeing. "No worries. What else?"

"Tell me why you threw away your title. I don't think I can take knowing it was because of me."

Remy turned in Aden's arms. When their gazes met, Aden sucked in a breath. He was staring at the real Remy for the first time in ages. "It was because of me," Remy said, and Aden could hear the truth in his words. "You're right. I wasn't me in Nevada. When you drew those awful stick people on our horse, I realized

181

something. I was never going to be me again as long as I held that title. Honest to god, Aden. The only thing I care about holding ever again is you." Aden swore Remy didn't blink as he continued. "The day of my match, when we were in that tub together, I searched my mind, praying I wouldn't forget to tell you everything I need you to hear. As I dipped into that ring, I realized I'd forgotten to say something I can't live without you knowing."

Aden caught himself holding his breath.

Remy held tighter to his waist. "I forgive you."

Aden's throat swelled. Remy meant it. Not once had Aden believed he'd ever hear those words from Remy. Now that he had, Aden knew he'd spend the rest of his life trying to earn them. Without thought, he slid the wetsuit lower, revealing more skin. "Without you, I'm less than half," Aden said, never meaning anything more in his life. "I also can't believe I'm saying this, but I'm about to fuck a dancing seal."

Remy untied the string on Aden's workout pants, proving he'd been busy while Aden had been distracted. "Damn right, you are."

In a flash, Aden had Remy's wetsuit peeled down to his ankles, and the man bent over the back of the couch. They'd always been explosive together. Today was no different. Aden brought his fingers to his mouth, wetting them before using them to stretch Remy's asshole. By the time he pressed inside Remy's body, Aden was already chanting his love and begging Remy to never leave. As Remy's tight ass squeezed Aden's cock, a sense of peace settled over Aden. This man was his—forever. Aden hadn't earned him, but he would. For the rest of Remy's life, he'd know he was Aden's heart.

Chapter 9

"You've been sent here because Drew thinks each of you has a real shot at the title. There's more to winning than you've been taught at No Rival. All of us standing before you are experts in our in fields. Obviously, I'm here to perfect your technique, but you need to learn more than how to fight. You need mental preparation as well. That's where Remy comes in. I think most of you have met him." Aden eyed the men's faces, searching for any sign they weren't following. They all looked ready to get on with things, so he continued.

"As the former welterweight champion, Remy can tell you more about the pressure you'll be under once you win than anyone else. Drew and I have decided that's knowledge you need before you decide to move forward with this dream. So, for the next two weeks, you'll be on rotation. Every day, you'll take turns working one on one with Remy." Several of the men exchanged smiles, obviously excited about training with one of the best. Aden didn't see the sense in disabusing their thoughts. In truth, they'd spend time goofing off with Remy, learning how to still have fun and not take this career choice so seriously while he also snuck in tidbits of information about the realities of the pressures of success.

Aden motioned Daniel's way. "If you haven't met Daniel, Mr. Long is a reporter for *The Daily Sports Report*. He will also be part of your rotation schedule."

"What can a reporter teach us?" Isaac asked, interrupting Aden's speech. Aden's gaze slid the man's way. In Vegas, Aden had noticed the chocolate-skinned male seemed a little less serious than most. Before now, he hadn't thought the man to be a training snob. Isaac shifted, looking uncomfortable beneath Aden's stare.

"Mr. Long..."

"I've come a long way from 'little bastard,'" Daniel said with laughter lacing his words. Aden ignored his interruption.

"... is a little bastard..."

Daniel snorted. "Ah. There it is."

"... but he's a professional. Unlike the tabloid rats you'll find surrounding you if you win the title, he'll only write the truth."

"Thank you for that," Daniel said.

Aden continued pretending Daniel wasn't trying to speak. "But the truth still may be more than you want the public to know. So Daniel will show you what to

185

watch for during an interview. Much to the detriment of his career, he can teach you how to guard your private life from the press while still giving enough quality information to keep people talking. Now," Aden said, ready to get started. "Since you spoke up, Isaac, I assume you don't mind taking the first turn with Daniel today."

The man's amber gaze slid Daniel's way. "That's cool with me."

Aden nodded and switched his focus Carter's way. "Carter, since you're already the most familiar with working with Remy, you'll be the first on rotation with him."

With a nod, Carter moved to join Remy. The pair headed for the door. Aden already knew Remy's plans for the man. What Carter needed most was to take a day off. The man took fighting way too seriously. If he ever made it to the top, Carter would fold in under a year if he didn't learn to find value in something else. To that end, Remy would give the man directions to a fishing boat that was leaving in two hours. Carter would be on that boat. He could get some fishing in or just enjoy the ride. Either way, he needed some time out on the water without distractions and far away from any training facility.

Giving his attention to the rest of the group, he waved for the men to follow him. "As for the rest of you, you'll spend your first day with Gunnar." A happy rumble of chatter erupted at his back. It wasn't every day someone in their position got to train with the world heavyweight boxing champion. "He'll be assessing your skills today. Tomorrow, the real training will begin."

The men split into groups. Gunnar handed out assignments while Aden supervised. He caught sight of Remy moving through the center sans Carter. He'd obviously already sent the man on his way. Pride and happiness welled in Aden's chest as he watched the man he loved chatting with everyone he passed. His smile was infectious. Everyone he spoke with laughed; even after Remy walked away, they continued smiling. They'd gotten married the day after Remy had shown up in Key Largo. It had been six months and Aden still had trouble not closing down early each day so he could enjoy his husband. Luckily, Gunnar had loved his time filling in for Aden while Aden has been in Vegas. He'd been easy to convince to come onboard for a joint venture with Aden and Drew, allowing Aden more time at home with Remy.

As if he felt Aden's stare, Remy glanced his way. Their gazes met. Remy's expression turned wicked.

Aden watched as Remy picked up the nearest phone and switched it to intercom.

"Aden, you're needed in the office."

Aden bit his bottom lip to keep from smiling. It was hard holding a serious expression as he headed for his office. Remy turned away, moving for the office as well. Aden's gaze dropped to the man's ass. Damn, he was a lucky man. Remy slipped inside, stealing Aden's visual feast. Aden picked up his pace. He didn't want to miss a moment with Remy. When he cleared the doorway, he found Remy sitting on his desk.

"You called?" Aden asked, trying to hide the hunger in his voice.

"I did," Remy said with a nod. "Crossfit Chad needs to have a real chat with you about today's schedule."

The smile exploding across Aden's face was out of his control. He closed the door behind him and quietly turned the lock. "Is that so?"

Remy nodded.

Aden moved closer until Remy had to tilt his chin up to hold his stare. "Do you have a problem with the way I schedule things around here?"

He was too busy enjoying the sight of Remy's gorgeous eyes, coated in smoky color, to notice Remy's fingers had twined their way around the string of

Aden's workout pants. He tugged, untying them.

"Crossfit Chad can't help but notice a serious oversight in today's plans."

Aden's mouth went dry. His dick stirred, already hardening. "I'm listening."

Remy's fingers curled around Aden's waistband. He slid the material down while never breaking eye contact. "When I looked over your schedule, it didn't have a time assigned for Crossfit Chad to rock your world."

Jesus. He loved this man. "That's because he already does, every second of the day."

A smile exploded across Remy's face.

Aden shuffled closer, forcing Remy onto his back. As Aden snagged the man's shorts and worked them down his hips, he tried to keep Remy's smile in place. "Don't tell Chef Charlie. He's the jealous type."

"And he owns knives," Remy added, sounding breathless.

"There's that too," Aden agreed as he dipped his head and kissed Remy's hipbone. His eyes fell closed as Remy's fingers ran through his hair. When he'd fallen in love with a brawler, he'd never expected he'd need the man's fighting spirit so goddamn much—not only to keep them together but to keep Aden from falling apart. Every day, Aden woke up vowing he would never let Remy down. Right now, he would do his part in keeping that promise. Remy wasn't getting down from this desk until Aden ensured the man couldn't walk through the club without blushing. He wanted everyone to hear Remy scream his name. They all needed to know what was important in life. It wasn't winning the next match. Life was about winning your soul's match.

The End.

Keep an eye out for the next installment in the Low Blow series, *Upstart.*

ABOUT THE AUTHOR

Charity Parkerson is an award winning and multi-published author with several companies. Born with no filter from her brain to her mouth, she decided to take this odd quirk and insert it in her characters.

*2015 Readers' Favorite Award Winner
*Winner of 2, 2014 Readers' Favorite Awards
*2015 Passionate Plume Award Finalist
*2013 Readers' Favorite Award Winner
*2013 Reviewers' Choice Award Winner
*2012 ARRA Finalist for Favorite Paranormal Romance
*Five-time winner of The Mistress of the Darkpath

Connect with her online:

--Website: charityparkerson.com
--Facebook: facebook.com/authorCharityParkerson
facebook.com/TheMenofSin
--Twitter: twitter.com/CharityParkerso

www.ingramcontent.com/pod-product-compliance
Lightning Source LLC
Chambersburg PA
CBHW060221180626

46813CB00007B/2909